D1094485

SPIN

SPIN

REBECCA CAPRARA

atheneum

NEW YORK LONDON TORONTO SYDNEY NEW DELHI

atheneum

An imprint of Simon & Schuster Children's Publishing Division
1230 Avenue of the Americas, New York, New York 10020
For information about special discounts for bulk purchases, please contact Simon & Schuster Special Sales at 1-866-506-1949 or business@simonandschuster.com.
The Simon & Schuster Speakers Bureau can bring authors to your live event. For more information or to book an event, contact the Simon & Schuster Speakers Bureau at 1-866-248-3049 or visit our website at www.simonspeakers.com.
Interior design by Irene Metaxatos
The text for this book was set in Fournier MT Std.
Manufactured in the United States of America
First Edition
10 9 8 7 6 5 4 3 2 1
CIP data for this book is available from the Library of Congress.
ISBN 9781665906197
ISBN 9781665906210 (ebook)

For my mother

PART I

Selvedge

I am not
 princess,
 nymph,
 demigod.

I am not
 beautiful,
 rich,
 educated.

I have no
 divine blood,
 noble connections,
 patron goddess.

I am Arachne.
 Known for my skill alone.
 And for that
 I am proud.

 Too proud, some say, snickering
 when I turn my back.

The verses and myths
all agree: hubris
leads to my demise.

But the bards and poets
often get it wrong, especially
when they speak of
girls and women.

So I will tell you
my version
of the story
and let you decide.

Warp

1.

An early memory,
warmly toasted and softened
around the edges by time:

Spin, my child, spin.

If I close my eyes,
I can hear
my mother's voice,
melodic
bright
like water splashing
from a fountain.

I can see her face,
eyes crinkled
in the corners,
olive flecked with amber.
Loose waves of dark hair
falling past her shoulders.

She claps.

Her hands are calloused
from hours at the loom,
fingers stained at the tips
from the herbs
she picks and grinds.

She sings,
Spin, my child, spin.

My heels, freed
from their sandals,
bounce to the beat.
My toes enjoy
the cool press
of the stone floor
beneath them.

The music is a river
and I jump in.
It sweeps me up
in its quick current.

I laugh, clap, twirl.
Father would not approve
of such folly,
but he is still at work
down among the dye vats,
so Mother and I wear our joy
openly, without shame.

Spin, my child, spin.

My legs, unsteady
with youth, wobble
as I stomp and twist
round and round,
              round and
     round and   round and
         round.

My head delights
in the dizziness—
the loss of control
as the room unravels
in whorls of color and light.

High above,
a spider
     hangs
     in
     the
     air.

Spinning, like me.

     Is she dancing
     or hunting?
     Or both?

I balance on tiptoes,
chin raised, eyes wide
with fear and wonder.

My mother follows
the thread of my gaze
                    up.
            up
up

The spider descends
from the rafters
into the space between us,
her gossamer silk so fine
it is nearly invisible.

There, she floats, suspended
in the summer air
like a deity
among the dust motes.

I scream and duck.

Stop, Arachne. Look.
My mother rests a gentle hand
on my shoulder.

She is a fellow weaver.
See how she works?
With grace and utility
in perfect harmony.

We stare a moment longer.
The spider is grotesquely beautiful
and beautifully grotesque.

A marvel, isn't she?

My mother lifts her hand,
inviting the spider
onto her palm,
then places it outside
in a patch of sage and scrub.

Lots of flies near the sty, she tells the spider,
as though they are old friends.
Best to spin outdoors this time of year.

In the yard, our pigs snuffle,
scratching their bristled haunches
against the fence boards,
their troughs abuzz with insects.
Yes, the spider will feast well there.

I smile, glad to see it crawl away
and warmed by the kindness
my mother affords
even the smallest creatures.

Farther in the distance,
temples and altars
dot the Lydian hillside.
Incense burns;
slaughtered rams
spill their blood
for the gods and goddesses
we are meant to
adore and appease.

But more than
clever Athena,
swift Hermes, or
pretty Aphrodite,
it is my mother
I admire most
in the world.

2.

I only dance
within the walls
of our humble home,
for my legs grow curved
as an archer's bow.

I will never be graceful
like the nymphs
who sway and bend as easily
as willow branches
to the sounds of lutes and lyres.

My gait is ungainly,
but my arms and hands
are strong and capable.

I can climb a tree
with impressive speed.
It is a useless skill,
  especially for a girl,
yet it brings me
great satisfaction.

When I prepare to climb,
I knot my skirts around my crooked knees
and plait my hair into tight braids,
to keep it from falling into my eyes.

I test the strength of each branch
as I ascend, avoiding weak or rotten limbs,
to keep myself from smashing
onto the ground below.

There, high amid the boughs,
I discover troves of acorns,
delicate birds' nests,
sprawling views of the Lydian hills,
and an intoxicating sense of freedom.

3.

Food is sometimes scarce at our table,
but my mother never runs out of stories.

I love hearing about Jason's Golden Fleece,
the maze-entrapped Minotaur,
the one-eyed Cyclops.

A bard travels to Hyponia from time to time
to sing in our village square.
I enjoy his tales,
but they're not as good as Mother's.
He often mixes up
the monsters and the heroes.

4.

A memory, burned at the edges,
tasting of soured milk and shame:

We visit the market where Mother trades
cloth and herb salves for meat,
briny olives, dried beans.

It is loud, crowded, too hot.
The air is heavy with the scent
of sweat, overripe fruit, salted fish.

Wagon wheels kick up dust.
Mules leave their droppings
in the street. A feral dog barks.

My eyes sting;
my nose burns.

I cling to my mother's skirts,
timid, only six years of age.

A woman catches my mother's attention
from across the crowded stalls,
her features obscured by a pale shawl.

She adjusts the fabric
ever so briefly, revealing
pleading eyes and
angry boils rising
from her cheekbones.

It is unclear whether she has been burned
or if disease mars her face.
Regardless of the cause,
my mother seems determined to help.

She retrieves a small clay jar
from inside her basket.

Wait here, Arachne.
I will return in a moment, Mother says,
giving a subtle nod to the veiled woman,
who bows her head gratefully
before slipping like a shadow
into an uncrowded alley.

I do not want to stand alone
amid the noise and heat,
but Mother says some wares
must be traded quietly,
beyond the prying eyes
of the gossiping marketplace.

Go fetch some figs or dates,
she says, pressing a coin into my palm.

I don't want to leave her side,
but I do love the sticky sweetness
of dried dates.

  What a strange, sickly child.
  The cooper gawks as I pass.

A scrap of a girl,
more skittish than a mouse,
the fishmonger agrees.

> *Her eyes, too large.*
> *Her nose, poorly shaped.*

I hurry through the aisles,
humiliation and bile rising
in my throat.

> *Look how oddly she walks. . . .*

Sallow skin and thin lips, too.
What a shame, the tanner clucks.

> *And such dull hair, dark as coal.*

No future, that one.

I smolder like an ember inside,
but stay quiet, too shy
and ashamed
to respond or fight back.

I hang my head and
quicken my pace,
avoiding their glances,
dodging the words
they hurl like rocks
in hushed whispers
that they think
I cannot hear.

5.

When we return home,
I tell my mother what happened
during our brief separation
in the market.

My bottled-up emotions
spill freely now;
my eyes become two rivers.

*Much as I wish I could,
I cannot shield you
from the world forever,* Mother says,
rubbing my back
as I cry into her lap.

*Nor can I spare you
the insults of others.*

Are they right? I croak.

*Of course not!
Pay them no mind, dearest one.
None at all.*

Still, I cannot forget
the things the villagers said. I feel
tender as a fig, soft-skinned and
easily bruised.

෬෮

I remember when you were born, Mother recalls,
attempting to cheer me with a tale.

You were a scrawny little thing,
no heavier than a small sack of grain.

I frown and draw away, but she pulls me back
into a loving embrace.

The midwife said you would not survive a week.
At this, you screamed defiantly, your tiny face red with fury.

The midwife was horrified by your howling. But me?
I was relieved to see you full of breath.

"A powerful voice does not serve a girl well," the midwife said.
Mother looks at me thoughtfully. *I disagree.*

Don't let fools define you, Arachne.
Don't let others speak for you.

She wipes my tears,
squeezes my hand.

I cannot teach you to read or write,
for these are gifts I do not possess, she says.

But there are other ways
to make your voice heard.

She walks to the loom, pulls a stool beside
her weaving chair, and invites me to join her.

6.

Our loom was not designed
by Daedalus, the brilliant inventor
of waxen wing and labyrinth fame.
It was crafted by my grandfather,
a boatbuilder, who spared a few boards
so that my grandmother could clothe
their eight children
in something better than rags.

The loom is not gilded,
or inlaid with mother-of-pearl.
She is plain and sturdy,
her wooden frame
made of old ship parts
and broken oars.

She boasts no intricate carvings,
only scuffs and scratches.

Her upper beam bears
faint circular scars—memories
of barnacles long since scraped away,
or perhaps kisses left by mermaids.
To me, these strange sea-marks
are more exquisite
than any decoration.

She has a personality, too.
When summer humidity settles,
thick as a damp blanket,
the loom grows stubborn

and temperamental,
refusing to budge
without ample coddling and coaxing.

In the winter months,
when bitter winds chatter our teeth,
the loom creaks and groans,
unhappy until her joints
are warmed and oiled
by my mother's patient hands.

7.

At the loom,
my mother's posture
is relaxed but sure.
She thumbs the threads,
adjusts the beam,
readies the warp.

After a minute or two
she falls into an easy rhythm,
the shuttle chattering quietly
as she passes it back and forth
between her palms.

The loom weights sway
as she ties in strings of
ochre, cream, pale yellow,
deep umber, jade, onyx.

I have seen my mother weave
countless times before,
but never quite like this.

I watch carefully,
absorbing each detail.

Row by row,
an image emerges in the cloth:
> An emerald-leafed tree
> with a dark-haired girl
> swinging from its branches.

Is that me? I ask, gazing
at her creation with wonder.

She nods, a smile quirking her lips.
Her fingers fly now, rapid as coursers.

My heart lightens,
the sadness and hurt
I gathered at the market
sloughing away.

Normally, my mother weaves
simple, durable cloth for
bandages, swaddles, bedsheets—
life's necessary, mundane vestures.

This is different.
Today she is painting with wool,

writing with thread,
singing with her shuttle.

Becoming a bard
in her own right.

And in doing so
she becomes
powerful.

I am seized by a strange sensation.
I don't have a name for the way I feel
and I struggle to contain
this surge of energy.

I fidget, unable to remain still.
My mother does not scold me;
she merely pauses her work
and points out the window.

A large oak tree stands
at the far edge of the field,
its branches outstretched
as though welcoming me
into a leafy embrace.

Go and play outdoors, Arachne.
The loom will be here
when you are ready.

Alas, this is not the day
I learn to weave.

But it is the day
I learn to set my gaze upward,
and lift myself
off the ground,
to reach toward
something, someplace
higher.

Never again content
to remain tethered
to the ground.

8.

When my mother is not weaving
and I am not climbing trees,
she and I spend hours
tending to our vegetables,
milking our lone goat,
feeding the pigs in the sty.

Not all of us can subsist
on ambrosia and adoration
like the gods.

Once our work in the garden is done,
we explore the woods beyond our pasture
where wild herbs and flowers grow.

Mother guides me
between dagger-shaped cypress,
across muddy streams,
over rocky outcrops.

She shows me
which roots to dig,
which berries to avoid,
and which knobbly olive trees
are hundreds, maybe even thousands, of years old.
These she treats like cherished ancestors,
pressing her palms reverently to their arthritic forms.

We pause to greet
insects, toads, serpents.
All manner of biting, warty, slithering things
grow docile when Mother is near.
My fear of these creatures fades to fascination.

I feel more welcome in their company
than I do among most people.

∽∾

We stop at a marble temple
nestled into the hillside.

The searing afternoon heat
blurs the horizon,
but the air inside
is cool and dry.

Mother places a woven peplos
upon the feet of the statue,
an offering for Athena,
goddess of wisdom, war,
and weaving.

The stone is so expertly carved,
so surprisingly luminous,
that I almost expect the sculpture
to come alive.

I imagine the owl on Athena's shoulder
taking flight, swooping low
and silent on broad hunter's wings.

I recall the bard's tales
of the goddess's contest with Poseidon
over the future of Athens.
I wonder at the power
of her shining aegis and spear.
I marvel at her cleverness,
her fearlessness.

What mettle Athena must possess
to challenge the sea god!

I hold the statue's frozen gaze,
waiting for her eyes to flash
with a flinty glare.

My chest swells with a mix
of admiration and fear.

I pray that she may grant me
a small portion of her courage.

I close my eyes
and wait.

A lazy breeze snakes
through the temple,
diffusing the heady sweetness
of burning incense.

I open my eyes,
my vision adjusting
to the waning light.

The goddess does not appear before me.
The altar remains unchanged.

I, too, remain unchanged.
I feel no divine infusion
of confidence or strength.
My prayer, unanswered or unheard.

Perhaps I am too impatient.
A lowly mortal, too unimportant.
Or perhaps the bard's tales
are myth alone.

I leave the temple
with an emptiness
in my chest
and deep hunger
gnawing at my gut.

I think of the bread we could buy
with Mother's cloth.
I do not understand
why she leaves her best work
at the soulless feet
of a statue. It seems to me
a terrible waste.

9.

Back at home,
we unload the contents of our baskets
onto the large kitchen table.

We pound earth-smelling roots into paste.
We dry racks of green herbs in the breeze.
We press strips of bark between flat stones
until they weep bitter tannins.

My mother blends these raw ingredients
with wine, honey, sharp vinegar,
whispering and humming all the while.

The mixtures become
tinctures, balms, and poultices,
which we sell at the market
for a pittance. It may not be much,
but it helps during lean times,
of which there are many.

Mother's pharmaka is only intended
to numb pain, disinfect wounds, fade scars.

Yet that doesn't stop villagers
from seeking her out
in shadowed alleys
where they beg her to brew
more potent draughts.

No matter how many coins they offer,
Mother insists
she does not possess the power
to make a nymph swoon, or
to heal a broken heart.

And I believe her. I think. . . .

10.

In his daily work,
my father performs
a different sort of magic—
taking dull, beige wool
and infusing it with color.

Unlike Mother, who smells
of herbs and wildflowers,
Father comes home each night
crusted with sea salt,
reeking of rotting fish.

His arms are stained and sinewy,
his back hunched from toiling
over the stinking pigment vats
clustered along the Lydian coastline.

No matter how much he bathes,
the stench of his work lingers,
seeping through his clothes, his skin,
maybe even his bones.

He is a dyer of purple—
a rare, regal hue.

The wealthy drape themselves
in its plum lushness,
unaware—or uncaring—of the methods
required to saturate their robes
with such brilliant, shocking color.

11.

Violet begins with violence.

I learn this truth
when Mother brings me to the shore
to watch Father work.

I find the process
both captivating and gruesome,
as creation and transformation
so often are.

Fishermen haul thousands
of tiny, spiraled mollusks from the waves.

Boys wield mallets and rocks,
pounding and smashing the shells

until inner glands burst
and juices flow.

Father gathers the macerated remains
to boil with wood ash and water
in lead vats.

He shields the mixture from light,
and leaves it to ferment
for a half-moon.

When the dye is ready,
an ungodly stench
rises from the vats.

Even the most seasoned dyers
cannot help but gag and retch
when the lids lift.

My father plunges carded wool
and bundles of combed flax
into the cloudy liquid.

After a few minutes,
he removes the dripping clumps
and hangs them to dry.

Exposed to air,
the thirsty fibers darken like an angry bruise
from light blue-ish green
to pomegranate, iris, amethyst.

Depending on the quality of the dye,
          and the whims of the gods,
my father occasionally produces
Tyrian purple—a blackish clotted-blood color,
prized above all others.

Following these fortuitous occurrences,
we eat well for several days,
gorging ourselves
on salty white cheese, hearty bread,
figs drizzled with amber honey,
and rosemary roasted mutton.

I forgive my father
the stench of his hands
and the brutality of his work
when we feast like this.

12.

A memory, sweet
as a sun-warmed pear:

I am eight years old,
up at dawn
to milk our goat.

I discover a wisp of a girl
just beyond the goat pen,
asleep in the dewy grass.

Father said a new family
moved down the road.
He did not say
one of them might end up
sleeping in our pasture.

The flaxen-haired girl wakes,
confesses she slept under the stars
because the grass here is so soft
and her newborn sisters
are so loud, wailing
with colic at night.
She hopes I am not mad.

How could I be mad?

Lonely and homely,
bereft of siblings and
ostracized by the children
I encounter at the market,
I have longed for a friend
for as long as I can remember.

Celandine, she says shyly,
telling me her name.

She is, I decide, a miracle.
A girl my age, who doesn't
gawk at my ungraceful gait
or unbeautiful features.
Whose smile is as bright

as the yellow flower
after which she is named.

Her stomach growls loudly.
She wraps her arms
across her slight waist,
embarrassed.

Come inside for breakfast, I say.
We have some bread to spare.
And soon I'll have fresh milk.
I hold up the wooden pail.

Oh, no. I couldn't bother your family
for food, she says politely,
in spite of her grumbling belly.

It's no trouble at all, I reassure her.

She shakes her head,
looks off into the distance.

There are pears in that tree, Celandine says,
pointing to the orchard that runs along
the edge of her property.
But they are too high to reach.

I smile. *I will get them for you.*
Finally, my climbing
proves useful.

After that first shared pear,
our friendship is instant
and easy. I do not judge the way
juice dribbles down her chin;
hunger is no stranger to me.

I join her, savoring
the last of summer's fruit,
forgetting to milk the bleating goat
until well past sunrise.

13.

A baby grows
in my mother's womb.

I can tell at first
by the flush of her cheeks,
and the roots she eats
straight from the garden,
known to quell nausea.

I try to ignore these signs.
After so many losses,
        at least one each year
        since I can remember,
I have learned
to cradle hope
in my heart
as delicately
as I might hold

a broken-winged bird,
understanding it will likely
never fly.

But as months pass,
the rise of Mother's bosom and
the swell of her stomach
are impossible to miss.

Maybe this time
will be different.

Even my hard-shelled father softens,
growing gentle and doting.

I do my best
to help where I can.
While Mother rests,
I scrub the dishes
and clean the floors.

Still, worry gathers like dust.
I do my best to sweep it away.

14.

One day, I slip out
into the meadow with Celandine
to collect sprigs of oleander,
which we twist into a wreath.

Despite my reservations, I offer
the circle of blossoms to Eileithyia,
the goddess of childbirth,
at her lichen-laced temple
in the woods.

Celandine promises
that a similar offering
ensured the healthy delivery
of her twin sisters last year.

Twins seem
incomprehensibly extravagant.
I would be happy
with just one
sibling to love.

I know Mother and Father
would too.

I explain all this
to Eileithyia
in silent prayer.

I hope
she's listening.

Knot

A story, told by Mother:

Daphne is a nymph who roams the woods.
Like we do, during our sojourns seeking herbs.
Daphne is content among the trees. Like you, my climbing girl.
She runs freely, with the wind in her hair.

Then Apollo arrives in the forest.
He startles Daphne and her friends, but they are not wary of him.
He isn't Hades, abductor of virgins and god of the dead.
Or Dionysus, raucous reveler, who plies unwitting nymphs
with wine until they are too drunk to protest.

No, Apollo is young and handsome.
The god of poetry, music, medicine.
How harmful could he be?

Daphne continues on her way.
Apollo, shot with Eros's arrow,
becomes mad with desire. He chases Daphne.

She runs as fast as a hare.
He pursues like a hound, his lust growing.

Daphne tires. If only she had a weapon,
or some small bit of power, she would turn on her heels
and run at Apollo. But she has neither.

"Help me escape!" she begs her father, the river god.

Peneus answers her call. Though not in the way she hopes.
The girl's muscles seize; her skin becomes encircled with bark.
Her hair changes to leaves, her arms to branches.
Her feet, once swift, root to the ground.

Daphne becomes a laurel tree.

Undeterred, Apollo kisses her bark,
wraps his arms around her trunk.

She shrinks from his unwanted touch.
She wants to scream, but she cannot.
Unable to run, hide, or fight,
she must endure
in unbearable silence.

15.

I think of the oak tree,
my favorite place to climb.

Were you once a maid?
I ask it one afternoon.

Did you ever run
from someone or something?
Do you mind me climbing
amid your boughs?
The tree, of course, does not respond.
Not with words, at least.

But its leaves rustle softly
as the breeze blows by,
and I think I hear it whisper
that I am welcome
within its arms.

16.

On warm nights
Celandine and I
spread blankets
upon the grassy knoll
where we first met.

We lie on our backs
beneath the stars,
finding stories
in their shapes.

My favorite constellations are
Callisto and Arcas—
big bear and small bear,
mother and child.

Celandine prefers Andromeda,
fair maiden rescued by noble Perseus
moments before the fearsome
sea monster Cetus devoured her.

Isn't it romantic? she sighs.

When I laugh
she turns serious.
*Only a love so pure and true
could be sewn into the stars,* she insists.

Sewn into the stars? I muse,
imagining a divine needle
stitching a love story
into the celestial fabric of the sky.

I lean back, gaze upward.
Thick clouds move east, tamping out
the glittering sparks of light.

The vast and sudden blackness
makes my head swim.

Celandine rolls to her side,
props her chin on her palm.
She smells of lavender and sea brine.

Even in the darkness,
her pale green eyes shine.
She is beautiful, but
she hasn't realized it yet.

We talk of things big and small,
sharing our hopes and dreams.

It strikes me that our lives
are like looms
awaiting whatever tapestries
we may yet weave.

In Celandine, I see
innumerable designs
and vibrant hues,
potential radiating
from each thread.

My own future
is less clear, although
Celandine says she is certain
I will find great fame
as a weaver, or at least
be remembered
as the best tree climber
in all of Lydia.

We sleep soundly on the grassy knoll,
enfolded in the velvety black,
soothed by the melody of crickets.

We are too young yet
to understand
that girls like us
rarely get to choose
the path and pattern
of our lives.

17.

Mother asks me to go to the market.
Her ankles are swollen and the walk is long.
I agree, but I do so reluctantly.

The village children whisper
louder, louder, taunting me
whenever I venture into town.

The boys run and tug at my hair,
kick rocks at my feet.

You should be grateful
they pay you any attention at all, the cooper's wife chortled
the last time the boys inflicted their cruelties.
Tears brimming in my eyes, I felt anything
but grateful.

I do my best to avoid them.

As soon as I step between the stalls
a gap-toothed boy calls out,
Here comes the spider girl!

He performs an exaggerated imitation
of my bow-legged walk
to a chorus of laughter.

I clutch my basket tightly. I clench my teeth.
I would flee, but scurrying away
is exactly what they want me to do,
and I do not wish to give them anything,
least of all satisfaction.

Above the market din
I catch the bard's warbling voice.
I pause to listen.

Suddenly, a sharp rock skitters across the ground,
striking my ankle painfully. I wince.
The gap-toothed boy snickers.

Across the square, the bard sings of heroes
lauded for bravery, fearlessness,
and strength. Emboldened, I turn
to face the boy. I narrow my eyes.

He cocks his head, bemused.
I have never stood up to him
or the others before.

Fury rises in me
like a squall.
Sudden, forceful,
tinting my vision red.

I pick up the stone at my feet
and throw it with surprising force.

The boy ducks just in time.
But the cart of fruit behind him
is not so lucky.

The vendor shouts, outraged
by the avalanche of apples.

It is her fault! the boy pronounces,
as though he is free of any blame.

I freeze. Just as quickly as it came,
my anger retreats, giving way
to a cold wash of regret.

A hush falls over the market.
I feel the weight of too many eyes
staring, the pressure of my ribs
constricting my pounding heart.

I try to explain, but no one listens.
Deep inside, I feel betrayed. Humiliated.
Worse, I feel powerless.

The vendor points at his damaged wares.
Reckless, stupid girl!
You will pay for this.

I hold up empty palms.
I have no more coins. *I cannot.*

You are the daughter of Idmon,
the purple dyer, are you not?

I nod, my cheeks aflame.

Your father will pay.
I'll make sure of it.
And if he's wise,
he'll beat you well.

Trembling, I turn to leave
and stumble over my own feet,
my ankle throbbing in protest.

The vendor watches with disdain.
He spits on the ground.
A girl like you is nothing
but a burden to her family.

18.

I cannot shake the incident in the market.

A girl like you is nothing.

The words sting and spread,
prickling my skin like a rash.

I dread encountering my father.
He has never been prone to violence,
but I have seen him swing a mallet at the shore,
bludgeoning shells against the rocks.

And I know that tavern wine
makes limbs loose and tempers bold.

Should he wish to beat me,
        as the fruit vendor threatened,
I shouldn't fare any better
than a helpless snail.

Thankfully, Father is not home when I return.

He has been experimenting
with new pigments,
spending longer hours at the dye vats,
hoping to bring in more money
before the baby arrives.

In the corner of the room
I discover a sack of colored fleeces
he has left behind.

In contrast to our home's dull palette
of gray and brown,
these hues are so brilliant
I nearly weep.

My dread dissipates,
the sting of the vendor's words fades.

Clutching a puff of saffron wool,
I imagine enrobing myself
in a shawl of pure sunshine.
I imagine a different, brighter life.

An idea hits me with the force
of a stone striking a cart of apples.

I run to find my mother.

I am ready to weave, I declare, eager
to help repay the debt of my outburst,
to avoid a beating,
to prove
I am not   nothing.

19.

Mother pulls the wool from my hands
and hangs it on the distaff.

Spin the wool first, Arachne.
And then we will see
if you are ready for the loom.

I have watched her so often
I feel as though I already know each step.

I feed the fibrous bundle
to the whale bone whorl,
watching as it wraps the spindle.

Careful now. Not too fast.

My fingers are hasty
and inexperienced.

The distaff droops.
The wool forms
ugly, uneven lumps.

Slow down, Arachne. Stop. Mother sighs.
She undoes my sloppy work.

Your craft must be worthy of the colors.

She makes me begin again.

I pout, frustrated and impatient.
For a fleeting moment
I find myself wishing
for a small dose
of divine intervention,
some meager assistance
from the goddess Athena.

It is too hard, I lament, after trying
and failing again.

The word
   nothing nothing nothing
rings in my ears, threatening
to swallow me whole.

It could be worse, Mother chides.
*Not all are so lucky
to toil with rainbows.*

I sit back, breathe,
think of Father's stinking vats.
I know my mother is right;
there is far worse work.

I pluck a fresh clump of beet pink wool
from the basket and begin anew.

Mother places her hands
over my own, guiding my fingers
slowly, slowly,
round and round.

She lets go. *Now you try.*

This time the wool
tightens and twists evenly.
The spindle fattens.

Mother nods.
This will make fine cloth.

I glow with pride
at this small achievement,
hoping it will be enough
to earn my father's forgiveness,
and surprised by how pleasant
the wool feels twisting
between my fingers.

I still have much to learn
but perhaps I can make something
of myself after all.

Mother sits beside me,
her hands resting atop
her growing stomach.

While I spin the wool,
she spins a tale.

Knot

A story, told by Mother:

There was once a young maid named Persephone,
so fair and sweet that flowers sprung up
each place her feet touched the fertile ground.
Her mother, Demeter, loved her very much.
Just as I love you, my child.

Hades—lonely god of the Underworld—
became smitten with Persephone. Desiring
a bride of his own, Hades implored his brother,
Persephone's own father, mighty Zeus himself,
to assist with her capture. Zeus agreed.

Shortly after, Hades kidnapped Persephone,
luring her with a single blossom, then cleaving
the earth beneath her, snatching the girl from her home
and family, despite her loud protestations.

In a cave nearby, Hecate—goddess of night
and magic—heard a terrible scream.
She searched for the source of the sound, but found nothing.
Helios, though he had witnessed the abduction, feigned ignorance.
Zeus, complicit in the crime, urged Hecate to halt her efforts.

But Hecate, suspecting something wicked
was afoot, would not relent.

When Demeter appeared days later, she was distraught.
Betrayed by her husband and bereaved of her beloved daughter,
she cried out in anguish. Hecate now understood
what had occurred. She agreed to help find the lost girl.

While Demeter's sorrow withered crops,
Hecate lit torches and conjured spells, commanding
the moon to shine brighter and brighter still.

You see, Arachne, darkness is everywhere.
But Hecate knew that the only way through it
was to shine a light.

So, she illuminated the dark, night after night, until
mother and daughter could be reunited.

20.

Is it true what the villagers say? Celandine ventures
one afternoon as we gather mushrooms.

Her twin sisters have caught a cold
and Mother asked us to collect ingredients
for a healing broth.

What do they say? I reply, kneeling
to watch a thin green snake
wind between the rocks.

I have not told her
what happened in the market,
fearing it will taint
her opinion of me, afraid I will lose
my best and only friend.

Some say that your mother is . . . a witch.
Celandine's eyes dart
to meet my own,
worried I will take offense.

I consider Celandine's question carefully.
I, too, have wondered about this possibility.
Not only when Mother coaxes cures from herbs,
but also when she recounts tales of sorceresses and witches—
     Hecate, Circe, Medea—
with the sort of reverence that the bards reserve
for mighty gods like Zeus.

My mother has a deep knowledge
of plants and the natural world.
Her draughts and balms are effective.

I pause and chew my lip, thinking.

But if she had any real magic,
she would surely use it
to dull the fermented fish stench
of Father's purpled hands.

At this, we both laugh.

Then my friend reaches out
and clasps my hand in hers.
She glances down knowingly
at the bruise darkening my ankle.

Gossip spreads swiftly, I suppose.

I cringe at the memory, but
with a reassuring squeeze of her hand
Celandine tells me
she is mine, still.

I squeeze back,
flooded with relief.

21.

My father does not beat nor reprimand me
for my behavior in the market.
Yet his displeasure is tangible,
expressed through cold stretches of silence.

If not for Mother's warmth,
this house would be unbearable.

The debt owed to the vendor
for the wares I damaged
weighs heavily.
I long to shake myself free
from the burden.

So, day after day,
I pull and comb
coarse clumps of fleece
between fine-toothed paddles
until the fibers transform
into soft, downy clouds.

These I spin,
filling spool after spool.

Mother gives gentle
but firm reminders:
*You must understand
the nature of your tools
and the elements of your craft.
Only then can you achieve mastery.*

And after mastery? I ask, overeager.

After mastery comes artistry, Mother replies.
But you must learn the rules
before testing their limits, Arachne.

Finally, after weeks of hard work
and seemingly endless spinning,
she invites me to weave
at the family loom.

Selvedge

Pause here for a moment—
  for this part of my tale
  is so often misconstrued.

When I finally learn to weave, there is
  no thunderbolt strike,
  no sudden communion with the Muses,
  no instant mastery of the loom.

Though it frustrates me
to hear my story told incorrectly,
I understand why
the poets take liberties
with these details.

They wish to impress the gods,
and secure their own places
in the memories of history.

And everyone knows
the gods find human toil
tedious, trivial, unbearably boring.

They much prefer
sweeping exploits of brave men,

thrilling tales of heroism,
blood-soaked battles,
amorous encounters,
and triumphant homeland returns.

When it comes to stories about
mortal girls and women,
they favor those featuring
      unparalleled grace,
      unrivaled beauty,
      unquestioning subservience.

The few who dare to challenge
or defy these expectations
are punished. Tongues slashed
from their mouths, robbed
of their own narratives,
yoked with the heavy mantle of
monster or villainess.

The unfairness of this
enrages me.

Which is one of the reasons
I spin my tale here, to set
the record straight.

22.

So here is the unglamorous truth of it:
When it comes to weaving,
I am not

a natural,
a phenom,
a prodigy.

I am clumsy.
I make countless mistakes.

I snarl the threads,
make a mess of the warp,
knock the loom weights together.

Mother is a patient teacher,
but she grants me no shortcuts.

Use your herbs, I beg.
Improve my skill, please!

She frowns.
*No tonic can cure
a distracted mind
or an impatient hand.
Tame your attention, child.*

Can't you use a spell? I huff,
recalling my conversation with Celandine,
wishing for witchcraft.

You want magic? Mother scoffs.
*Dedicate yourself to the craft,
and in time you will see
the magic of practice take root.*

I storm off
frustrated by my inability
to tie the most basic knots.

Outside, I inhale
fresh linden-scented air.

I run my palms along
feathered stalks of wheat.

I pluck a sprig of mint
from the garden
and chew its leaves.

I wander, letting my temper cool
and my agitated mind settle.

Seemingly of their own accord,
my feet carry me far across the hillside
toward Athena's temple.
I pause before it. My eyes follow
the fluted columns, rising formidably
from the dry earth toward the heavens.

I take a breath and step inside,
faith fluttering in my chest
like a butterfly drying newly formed wings.
I push aside my uncertainty and kneel.

I open my heart
and pray.

I have no figs, wine,
or lambs to slaughter.
Instead, I offer the contents
of my apron pockets:
a small handful of carded wool
and a tangled length of thread.

I lay these humble gifts
upon the altar
and bow my head,
as I have seen Mother do before.

I tell Athena of my struggles.
I implore her to assist me.
I wait, and pray,
and wait some more.

I am met with silence,
deep and hollow as a drum.
Disappointment pinches my chest,
but it is not enough to dissuade me.

Stubborn as a mule,
I return to the temple the next day
and the day after that,
bringing better offerings,
praying more earnestly than ever.

Despite my efforts, it becomes clear
that the goddess cannot be bothered
with the sorry likes of me.

Shunned or ignored,
doubt, anger, and mistrust
dampen the fragile wings of my faith
like dew, each droplet crystallizing
in the frigid chill
of the statue's unyielding gaze.

Eventually I return to the loom,
sheepishly asking my mother
for forgiveness and assistance.

Unlike Athena,
I know she will listen
when I speak.

23.

Sitting atop an uncomfortable stool,
I work for hours, days, weeks,
until my fingers ache and bleed.

My progress is slow,
but there are small victories.
The scintillating thrill of growth
and gentle encouragement from Mother
are just enough to sustain me.

Even then, I am barely
proficient, far from fluent
in the loom's elusive language.

Nevertheless, I try.

Spurred by the need to prove myself,
and increasingly captivated by the craft—
    which frustrates and fascinates me
    in equal measure—
I am drawn to the warp like a fly to a web,
unable to disentangle myself
from its tensile threads,
as though my life and loom
are somehow bound together,
preordained by the Fates themselves.

24.

I complete my first swath of fabric.
It is rough and imperfect.
I hide it from sight,
embarrassed by its flaws.

I make another,
and another after that,
practicing with whatever yarn
I can procure.

The shuttle, when wielded properly,
becomes an instrument of beauty
and an outlet for pent-up anger.

    A girl like you is nothing . . .

Immersing myself
in the shuttle's rhythmic *husha-hush*
drowns out unwelcome voices.

Mother oversees my work, but as I improve,
she interjects less and less,
leaving me to fix my own mistakes
and find my own rhythm.

As her stomach swells
she grows more and more tired,
my unborn brother or sister
sapping the energy from her.

Rest, I tell her, glad to feel useful.
I shall spin the flax
and weave the wool.

My debt to the fruit vendor
nearly paid, Father's coldness
toward me thaws.
Even so, I still have much
to prove.

25.

Mother asks me
to join her at the temple.

I have not returned
since my last failed attempts
at piety and devotion.

But I agree to accompany her,
content to be at her side
as we pick our way
through the woods,

stopping here and there to admire
bees and blossoms.

The temple is abuzz with activity.
Old women and sea-beaten fishermen
light incense and mutter prayers,
beseeching Athena for all manner of blessings.

A few children skip
between the columns.

Just beyond the stone steps, I spot
two nymphs whispering together.

Part maiden, part spirit,
and wholly beautiful;
it is rare to see these minor deities
of woods and water
among us lesser mortals.
Usually, they prefer wild places.

However, a lush forest
of linden, oak, and laurel trees,
as well as a gently winding brook,
and many mossy alcoves
encircle the temple clearing,
so perhaps the nymphs
feel comfortable here.

I pause to watch them, transfixed.

Their laughter is melodic,
their movement languid.

One of them encircles
the other's waist with her arm,
and they dance together
between the trees,
bodies pressed close.

Something inside me
flickers to life,
spreading warmth
along my limbs
and goosepimples
across my skin.

I realize I'm staring,
gawking even,
my neck and cheeks
reddening.

The nymphs dance
in plain view and yet I feel
like an interloper, intruding
upon a private moment.

I quickly dart inside the temple
and rejoin my mother.

She is there, kneeling,
setting a handful of sticky dates
on a broad green leaf
before the goddess.

Then she reaches into her basket
and pulls out a linen cloth.

She drapes it across
Athena's stone feet.

I made that, I say dumbly.

Yes, and it is fine work, daughter.

I do not wish to give it away, I say.
Not to her. I gesture at the statue.

Mother's eyes widen.
Her head snaps to see
if anyone else has heard
my impudent remark.

A crone in a gray headscarf
regards us with one eye;
the other eye is fogged
with cataract.

Mother grabs my arm,
pulls me outside.

What were you thinking? she hisses,
once we are a safe distance from the temple.

I am not used to seeing her
agitated like this.

*What has Athena
ever done for us?* I say defiantly,
recalling the times I wished

for the goddess's gifts,
for her very presence.
Every plea futile
and unanswered.

My mother sucks in a sharp breath.
She grips her stomach and winces,
as though my impiety wounds her.

Or, perhaps, the child growing inside
has delivered a swift kick.

As the pain dissipates,
her brow smooths.

She composes herself, then says,
For a clever girl,
you are terribly foolish.

Her voice becomes stern
as her hands wrap protectively
around her swollen belly.

Sometimes it is not
what the gods give us,
but what they spare us.

26.

I cannot sleep.
I lie in bed that night
mulling thoughts
like wine.

All this time,
I imagined
our temple visits
were meant
to bring us
closer
to the gods.

But perhaps
they were
truly intended
to keep us
        apart.

Knot

A story, remembered:

Aite is a daughter of Zeus. You may not hear of her often,
for the bards are reluctant to speak her name.

She was banished from Mount Olympus long ago.
A castaway, unwanted.

Why was she exiled? you ask.
As she came of age, Aite began to feel the pulse
of something powerful flow through her veins.
Not divinity, or lust, but something else.
Something akin to mischief.

As a child, she would tip over amphorae in the storehouse
just to see freshly pressed oil spill across the ground.
She would smash her brothers' wooden towers
just to watch the blocks tumble and hear the boys cry.

In time, what began as youthful troublemaking
took a dangerous turn. Her desire for destruction
became vast, uncontainable, uncontrollable.

Aite quickly mastered the art of manipulation,
bending others to her will, delighting
in the wreckage her lies and actions could cause.

She was so cunning, in fact,
that she eventually deceived her own father.
        (Of course, the ruse was Hera's idea,
            but that is a story for another day, my child.)

Zeus, outraged by his daughter's disrespect,
hurled her from the mountaintop.
        How dare she make him look like a fool?
        How dare she meddle with his desires?
        How dare she form an alliance with his wife?

Where is immortal Aite now? you ask.
Look around, and you will see
that the goddess of conflict, delusion, and ruin
wanders the earth among us,
wreaking havoc without remorse wherever she goes.

The Litai—her ancient sisters—trail her,
trying their best to make amends,
to clean up the debris, to heal
whatever or whomever
their younger sister breaks.

But they are never able to keep pace.

You see, my child,
the gods can provide many things:
They can bring crops to bloom,

shepherd babies safely
from their mothers' wombs,
guide lost travelers home.

A god can conjure
a boat during a storm.
Or a god can be the storm.
   And if they're anything like Aite,
   they might even enjoy it.

Beware, for with a snap of their mighty fingers
the gods can upend a mortal life.

27.

Celandine and I hang upside down
from the lower branches
of the oak tree.

The blood rushes
to our heads,
hair dangling
like seaweed.

Up here in the boughs
with my dearest friend by my side,
the wreckage and woes of the world
feel impossibly far away,
as though gods like Aite
could never touch
this happy spot.

Across the field,
my mother fills her basket
with rosemary and sage,
her face bathed in late-afternoon light.

I call to her and wave.

She bends awkwardly
to pick the herbs,
for her stomach is now as large
as a melon.

She stands and waves back at us,
then rubs her lower back,
her face contorting.

Even from this distance,
I can tell something is awry.
She cries out in pain
and drops to her knees.

Celandine and I swing down
from the tree and run,
the tall grasses tickling
our bare feet and shins.

We help ease Mother
onto a patch of moss.

Celandine is the eldest
of six brothers and sisters;
she recognizes the labor signs
immediately.
I will bring the midwife, she says.

She rises and races across the yard.
The wooden gate claps shut as she leaves.

Hurry! I shout after her,
feeling helpless and unprepared.

Is . . . is . . . is there a salve? I stammer.
To ease the pain?

Mother shakes her head
and holds my gaze.

Shall we move inside?
To your bed? I ask,
clutching her hand.

No. She grinds her teeth
as searing rigors
surge through her.

When they subside
for a brief moment
she mutters prayers
to Eileithyia.

Grant this child
safe passage
into the world.

Desperation replaces doubt.
I echo each word, trembling.

This is nature's way, she assures me.

But I am scared,
overwhelmed and confused
by the brutal, earth-rending
force of childbirth.

Mother grimaces.
The surges of pain
come quicker now.

I run inside to gather supplies.
Dry blankets, clean water.

Where is the midwife?
I scan the horizon.

Guttural sounds form deep
in my mother's throat.
I dab her forehead with a damp cloth.
She grunts and writhes away from me.

I fear that Eileithyia
hasn't heard our prayers.
I fear that the gods have chosen
to punish us
for some unknown sin.
Perhaps my past insolence
is to blame?

I am terrified
Mother will die
before my eyes
and I will be powerless
to stop it.

28.

When my brother emerges,
he is curled and wrinkled like a grub,
coated in blood and whitish paste.

Not at all
the rosy-cheeked cherub
I had imagined.

The midwife has not yet arrived,
so I lift him up
for my exhausted mother to see
and realize he is tangled—
> a rope of flesh
> knotted
> around his thin neck.

His skin darkens to the color of father's dyes:
an unsettling, unnatural purplish blue.

I scream and unwind the cord
as rapidly and gently as possible.

Mother reaches a finger into his tiny mouth
to clear out the thick birthing fluids.

She thumps him on the bottom. . . .
Finally, blessedly,
my brother wails!

His skin pinks.
His eyes open.

He sees me
and shrieks.

I have never been so grateful
to hear a baby cry.
I cry too.

Mother pulls him to her breast,
warming him against her bare skin.

She doesn't shush him right away.
She lets him exercise his lungs
a moment longer,
before offering her breast.

He takes it greedily
and begins to suckle,
as though it were
the most natural thing,
which, I suppose, it is.

He is a miracle, isn't he? Mother says, smitten.

I nod, awash with relief and awe.

We will call him Photis, she decides,
which means light.

29.

Despite his terrifying entrance
into the world,
my brother's name suits him.

His very presence brightens
the dim corners
of our home and hearts.

Even Father warms, lingering
around the hearth and table,
his mood uncommonly jovial.

When Photis coos and smiles,
my father radiates the sort of pride
that only a son can summon.

A single milky burp
from my brother's bow-shaped mouth
draws applause. Even gassy rumbles
are worthy of paternal praise.

Meanwhile, I labor at the loom,
struggle beneath the distaff,
and receive nary a grunt
for my efforts.

The injustice is not lost on me,
yet I do not hold this against my brother,
for he is only an innocent babe,
and his charms bewitch me as well.

30.

Perhaps because
I assisted with his birth,
my baby brother
imprints on me
like a duckling.

As soon as he learns to walk,
Photis toddles in my wake,
following me everywhere.

Downy and sweet,
his cheeks are kissably plump.
His hair forms a halo
of soft black curls.
His warm brown skin
impossibly soft.

Mother watches us together.
He adores you, Arachne.

I feel the same,
even when he tugs relentlessly
on the hems
of my skirts, begging,
Up, up, up!

I scoop him
into my arms
and spin him
round and round
while Mother claps
and sings.

Spinning,
        spinning,
the two of us giddy,
dizzy with delight.

Photis's laughter
pauses only when he demands,
More, more, more!

I find new ways to amuse him,
inventing games, dances, and songs,
savoring his smiles and wonder,
proud of each new thing he learns.

As he grows older and stronger,
Mother and Father allow me
to take Photis on small adventures
through the fields behind our home.

I show him my favorite places,
careful to keep him from harm
as we scramble over rocks,
dip our toes in shallow creek water,
rest beneath the large oak tree.

As time passes,
I struggle to remember
the days when Photis was not
part of our family,
so perfectly does he complement
our little group.

31.

Shortly after Photis's fourth birthday,
my mother wakes me

from a deep slumber
with an unusual request.

Rise, child, she whispers.
I need your help.

It is too early . . . or too late, I protest,
not knowing if it is day or night,
only knowing that I need more sleep.

Come, Arachne.
Mother pulls the sheets back.
Cold air pricks my skin.
I sit up and scowl.

We must leave now,
before Helios blots out
the full moon's light.

What? Why? I grumble.

One year ago, I spied an unusual herb
when I walked in the woods.
It was merely a sprout at the time,
too small to harvest.

Ever since, I've been watching. Waiting.
After all these months,
I believe it may finally bloom.

Does it help with muscle aches? Or warts? I ask groggily,
for these are the villagers' most common complaints
at the market.

No, nothing like that.
This is entirely different. . . .

Her voice trails off as she casts a look
at my father and brother,
both snoring in their beds.
Out the window,
the stars glimmer and wink.

Hurry, she says.
I will tell you more later.

There is urgency in her normally calm voice,
so I dress quickly and follow her outside,
closing the door soundlessly behind me.

⟊

The dew is cold and wet
beneath our feet.
I carry an empty basket and
two dry rolls for our breakfast.
My mother carries a linen pouch
and a curved blade.

The moon hangs
like a heavy pearl,
glowing so brightly
we don't require a torch.

Even so, I do not know
which direction we travel.
I am tired and disoriented

and my mother seems to
double back several times.

Finally, we stop
in the cool night shade
of a copse of trees.

Mother surveys the ground.
She inhales sharply,
then drops to her knees.
Here it is!
Help me, child.
Dig like this.

She works her fingers
deep into the soil.
I join at her side.

Careful now.
Get beneath the roots,
or else you'll sever
the bulb from the stem.
Don't bruise the petals.

I sink my hands into the earth,
more awake and alert now,
curious what plant could be so important
that we must harvest it under the cloak of twilight.

She lifts a milk white flower
with black roots from the dirt.

What is it? I ask,
pulling up a small bulb of my own.

Moly, she breathes, the word
like a smooth pebble
in her mouth.

This plant is very, very rare, Arachne.
She pauses. *And potent.*

I nod, not knowing what to say.
To me, it looks like a million other flowers,
pretty but unremarkable. Plus, this one smells
more like onions than lilies.

*Some believe it first sprouted from drops
of spilled giant's blood,* Mother explains.

I grimace at the thought.

*Others say it blooms only once a decade.
For a single night, during a full moon.*

I understand the urgency now,
her need to rouse me from sleep.

*Some believe its sap transformed
Scylla into a sea monster.
Many say that mortals will be struck dead
if they attempt to harvest it,* she adds.

I gasp, horrified.

But here we are, she says, brightening, very much alive.
She takes the moly from my hand.

The poets say many things, Arachne.
Their verses may delight your ears,
but you must learn to question
the stories you hear.

She whispers now,
her voice nearly inaudible,
in case Selene—driving her ivory chariot
and silvered horses across the domed sky overhead—
feels inclined to eavesdrop.

It does not always serve the gods
for us to know their truths.

I am shocked to hear
my mother speak this way.

She visits the temples every week,
piously laying offerings at the altars,
   in spite of my protests.

I never imagined
her heart brimmed
with rebellion.
   It is a great relief.

For I, too, find these god-pleasing gestures
perplexing, empty, frustratingly unrequited.
I derive far greater solace and wonder

from the natural world—
> the fluty whistle of an oriole,
> the elegant twist of a grapevine,
> the ingenuity of a spider's web.

My head spins, the axis around which
my mind previously rotated is now askew.
Perhaps it will never be righted. Perhaps that is all right.

I observe my mother. Her face, a familiar landscape
I've gazed upon thousands of times.
I've sought comfort in her smile,
discovered wisdom etched along her brow,
found laughter in her eyes.

I thought I knew her face—I thought I knew *her*—so well.
Yet, somehow, the moonlight, the moly, her whispered words
reveal new angles and hidden depths.

I feel dizzy, unmoored by the realization that
you can love someone your entire life
and they can still surprise you.

The moly, I say, collecting myself.
Will you use it for witchcraft?

She flinches.
I do not practice witchcraft.
Do not speak such nonsense, please.

I nod apologetically,
not wanting to anger her.

It is far too dangerous
for a mortal to peddle in magic.

Why? I ask, worry coating my throat.

She regards me thoughtfully
then answers with a question:
What makes a god afraid, Arachne?

To me, the gods have shown themselves to be
indifferent and untouchable.
I think for a long moment, gathering a litany of fears
and dangers in my mind:
        venomous serpents, raging storms, sharpened spears.
What harm or threat could any of those things pose
to a mighty, immortal being?

I do not know, I confess.

She responds gently but earnestly,
The only thing a god truly fears
is a power greater than their own.

Then she looks down at the plant in her hand.
She places it carefully in our basket
and covers it with a cloth.

What will *you do with the moly?* I ask.

Mother looks up, her expression shifting again.
In the moonlight, her eyes blaze
with an almost feral ferocity.

It is a look I have only seen once before,
when I encountered a she-wolf in the forest.

The animal snarled, bared her teeth;
a litter of pups rolled and wrestled behind her.
Her yellow eyes glowed. In them, I saw a mother
intent on protecting her young at all costs.

My mother blinks;
the fire in her eyes fades.
She shakes her head.
I am not sure just yet.
But one day, my sweet girl,
it might be of use.

One day, it might be
very important indeed.

Until then,
you must never utter a word
about this herb to anyone.

32.

Photis begs me to fight.

Just pretend, okay?
He hands me a wooden sword,
which is just an elmwood stick.

You can be Hector.
I shall be Achilles, he says,

jabbing the stick and
hopping like a locust.

What if I wish to be a girl warrior? I ask,
swinging my make-believe sword,
enjoying its weight in my hand.

Unless you are a goddess like Athena or Artemis,
there is no such thing! Photis rolls his eyes
at the absurdity of my query.

You can be a monster, like snake-maned Medusa, or . . .
He bites his lip, thinking. *Perhaps Helen,*
but she is so very beautiful, and . . .

I give my brother a playful whack
and make a hideous face.
What? Your imagination cannot stretch that far?

He laughs and stabs his sword in my direction.
Back, you beast! he roars.

We slip and dash
along the muddy riverbank,
jousting, jesting, laughing
until our sides split
and our feet are caked with mud.

33.

In the months after we harvest the moly,
Mother's storytelling changes,
focusing more and more on girls, like me.

Lately, after she finishes a tale—
        which never seem to end the way
        I think they should—
I simmer with emotion, clench my fists,
run and hide. Anger blossoms
into a fiery thing I struggle to contain.

The blame hefted upon Pandora,
the beheading of misunderstood Medusa—
these tales dredge up memories of the market,
of encounters and cruelties which grow
more numerous and unsettling
with each cycle of the moon.

I remember the rock I hurled, the one time
I fought back. So much disgrace and worry
accompanied my small act of rebellion.

Ajax, Achilles, Heracles are celebrated
for much worse—their violence and vengeance
revered as necessary, noble acts.

It seems that standing up for yourself
is a privilege reserved for men and gods.

⟋∞⟍

Mother comes to find me.
She rests a hand on my back.

You need not hide
your emotions from me, Arachne.
I am glad that you feel so deeply.
It tells me you are listening.

But anger is a complicated beast.
Around others, you must learn
to tame it, restrain it.
Yet never let yourself become numb to it.

I search her face for answers,
for it seems she speaks in contradictions.

When she sighs, her breath seems to carry
the exhaustion of millennia.
Guard your anger wisely, Arachne.
Gather it like a precious herb,
for there may come a time
when you will need to draw
great strength from it.

34.

Some girls, like Celandine,
come into womanhood
gracefully. Not I.

My transformation occurs
in fits and bursts,
my body a landscape
I no longer recognize.

Some mornings, without warning,
I awake to a new dip or swale,
a thickening here, a softening there.

Patches of dark hair,
oily spots along my brow,
musk beneath my arms.

When I seek my reflection
in the clear river water
I feel as though
I gaze upon a stranger.
A chimera caught
between woman and child,
an awkward, in-between creature.

I find beauty
in the bodies of others,
but the shifting terrain
of my own flesh
puzzles me, scares me,
sometimes even
repulses me.

I dislike the way my clothes cling
where they once flowed loosely.
I hunch my shoulders
to hide the rolling hills
rising defiantly
from the planes of my torso.

Look! You have finally caught up, Celandine says,
smoothing her hands across her own bosom.

I cannot help but blush.

I didn't know this was a footrace, I reply awkwardly,
feeling as though my skin
fits as poorly as my clothes.

You know I jest, dear friend, Celandine says,
throwing an arm around my shoulders.
You are perfect just as you are.

My breath catches
as I lean into her embrace,
wishing her words were true.

❧

Despite Celandine's kindness,
I struggle to accept
my ever-changing form.

Wary of attention,
I shy from people in town,
unable to read the intent in their eyes,
and unnerved by their curiosity
in whoever, or whatever, I am becoming.

Some days, when the village boys taunt me,
my blood simmers, my skin itches.
I long to disappear.

Instead, I sew a new dress
with more generous seams.
I loosen the apron strings
cinching my waist.

Then I weave a flowing shawl,
and wrap myself
in folds of fabric,
creating a cocoon
to hide within
until I am ready
to emerge.

35.

The weather turns as
seasons shift, bleeding
from one into another.

Winter winds blow inland
from the sea, tearing leaves
from the poplars, exposing
their slender branches,
glazing once-verdant fields
with stiff hoarfrost.

I clutch my shawl, pulling it tighter
across my shoulders, and hurry to market,
dreaming of hot broth and a warm bed.
I keep my eyes trained on the path,
vigilant for slick patches of ice.

A woolen headscarf protects my ears
from the biting wind, muffling
the sounds around me.

I am not prepared
when the boys approach.
I do not hear them coming.
I do not see them
until it is too late.

One shoves me from behind.
The other nudges me from the side.
I stumble, nearly twisting my ankle.

I steady myself
just in time
to feel their cold, cruel hands
pawing at my skirts,
lifting the layers of fabric
        higher, higher,
inviting the icy air to nip
at my bare flesh.

Let us see what you're hiding
beneath those skirts, spider girl!

Show us why you walk that way.

They leer and look.
The trespass of their eyes
fills me with shame and panic,
deep and awful. I retch
and push them away.

Come on, now. Don't be so shy.

I inhale sharply, goosepimples dimpling
my shocked skin. I scream and try
to tear myself free, like the leaves
liberated from their branches,
scattering in the howling wind.

But I am not swift enough.
The boys catch me, grabbing,
groping, their fingers like claws
on my calves, my knees, my thighs.

⌘

I lose my footing—
      I lose my sense of place—
            I lose my sense of time—
                  I lose my sense of self.
I am no longer
    a girl.
        I become
            a rabbit
pursued
by a predator—
      small,
          helpless,
              wild-eyed.
My heart beating
      frantic—
          frantic—
              frantic.
My brain's only signal:
    Get away!
        Get away!
            Get away or be eaten!

◦❦◦

I return to myself
and scramble to my feet.

Before I can flee,
the stockier boy knocks me
down again onto the frozen
unforgiving earth, eying me
like prey.

I am no longer cold;
my body blazes
with fury and disgust and
the heat of humiliation.
If I shiver, it is from fear alone.

My mother's a witch, you know! I scream,
terrified and desperate, pulling
my skirts down to cover my legs.

Touch me again and she will curse you!
I swear it! Spittle flies from my mouth.

My words give them pause.
The taller boy scowls.
The stockier boy squints.

Mother forbade me
from speaking of witchcraft,
but its promise is the only weapon
I wield right now, so I shout louder,
Leave me be, or be cursed!

The tall one regards me a moment longer,
then breaks into laughter, mocking and menacing.
The other boy joins in, as though their attack
was all in jest. As though I would be mad
to think otherwise.

36.

As quickly as they appeared,
the boys are gone again.

For a moment, alone on the path,
I question my own sanity.
Did I imagine it all?

No, I did not.

Long after they leave
I can still feel
their eyes and hands
on my body.

I can still hear
their laughter
roaring and ringing
in my ears.

Bruises bloom
on my hip, my elbow,
where I struck the earth
when they shoved me down.

If I had not threatened them
with a curse,
how much further
would they have taken their abuse?

With shaking hands,
I rewrap my scarf,
trying to silence the sounds,
to erase the memory,
but it is impossible
to forget.

37.

I want to go home,
but if I return
without the market goods
Mother will demand
an explanation,
and I cannot bear to speak
of what happened.
Not to her, or Celandine, or anyone.
Not when this shame
still burns like a brand.

I force the pain aside
and continue onward.
What other choice do I have?

During the long, frigid walk to town,
I seek comfort in stories.

I think of a tale the bard once told,
about Artemis and the stag:

> A man named Actaeon went out on a hunt.
> Deep in the woods, he heard women's voices.
> Curious, he snuck closer, surprised to spy Artemis
> bathing in a spring, attended by nymphs.
> He gazed upon the goddess for some time
> before being discovered.
>
> Outraged and embarrassed
> that he had seen her naked,
> Artemis punished Actaeon
> by turning him into a stag.

I laughed years ago, when I first heard that part,
envisioning a man sprouting antlers and hooves,
delighting in the creative transfigurements
the gods could inflict when angered or insulted.

But I stopped laughing when I learned
that shortly after he became a stag,
Actaeon was torn to pieces by his own hunting dogs,
as commanded by furious Artemis.

I frowned and pouted
at the unfairness I perceived.
Surely this punishment
did not equal the crime.
I felt badly for Actaeon.
I was mad at Artemis.

I understand now
how wrong I was
to judge her.

38.

A memory, honeyed
but bitingly tart:

Celandine and I
allow Photis to join us
in the forest.

We scour the ground for wild berries,
which stain our lips the same shades
that Father conjures in his dye vats.

Photis skips at our heels,
following us
over rock and ridge.

We pause
at my favorite climbing tree—
the gnarled oak,
studded with acorns,
knobs of twisted bark,
and ruffles of crimson leaves.

The best acorns are up high, I tell them.
I will gather some for Mother.

I'll help! Photis declares.

No. You stay there, I instruct my brother,
pointing to the ground.

He whines and stomps his feet.

You are too young
to climb so high.
If you are hurt,
Mother will be very cross.

I ascend, savoring the view.
I may not enjoy this freedom
much longer; climbing
does not suit girls
of marriageable age,
a destination which I seem to be
rapidly, yet unwillingly, approaching
even though I am barely fourteen.

But I feel safe up here,
far away
from the eyes of the village.

Photis sulks. Even in his misery,
his round face is dear.
He sniffles, wiping his nose
with the back of his hand.

I cannot bear to see him upset.
I stuff my pockets
with a few handfuls of acorns
then sigh and climb down.

Let us find some more berries
to cheer you, brother, I say.

He only scowls and
digs in his heels.

Come along, Celandine says warmly,
taking his hand in hers.

I cannot ply him with berries,
but a smile from Celandine
does the trick.

As we leave the meadow
I catch Photis
casting long looks
over his shoulder
at the mighty tree,
as though it is a foe
he longs to vanquish.

39.

Photis is not the only one
smitten with Celandine.

Her flaxen curls,
petal pink mouth,
newly rounded hips
draw the gaze
of boys and men
whenever we pass
through the village square.

Their eyes rove
across her body,
like she is a ripe pear
ready for picking.

I sneer at them
and bare my teeth,
my temper flaring.

Celandine swats my arm and laughs.
It's harmless flattery, she says, cheeks flushed rose.

But I know a different story,
one I'd like to spare my friend.

Aw, ugly Arachne's just jealous, someone teases.

They are wrong. I do not envy
my friend's charms, her looks,
the attention she receives.
I have never coveted these things.
To me, they are only secondary.
For I know her heart,
which is more beautiful still.

So I will spit and sneer
and fight if I must
to protect her
from the humiliation and hurt
I carry silently
inside.

40.

Look! Look at me, Arachne!
Am I not brave?
Photis runs and tumbles
through the forest, undaunted
by the lengthening shadows
of late afternoon.

Oh, yes, I acquiesce, watching him
with a bemused smile, a half-full basket
swinging in the crook of my arm.
You are the bravest.

He leaps over a large rock.
Look how nimble and swift I am!

Indeed. The swiftest!
Did you steal Hermes's sandals, brother?

His delighted laughter
warbles like birdsong.

He dashes ahead of me on the trail.
He lifts one end of a rotted log,
his thin arms quivering under its heft.
He looks at me with expectant eyes.

And the mightiest! I declare.

Satisfied, he drops the log
to the ground with a terrific *thump!*
Troves of hidden insects scatter.

Don't stomp on them! I insist,
watching the skittering beetles and wriggling worms
as they seek shelter from the sole of Photis's boot.
Thankfully, my brother complies.

A hero, not only courageous,
but compassionate, too! I proclaim.

Photis plants his hands
upon his hips and exhales loudly,
the posture of a man
on the frame of a boy.

How easily he wears his pride,
how naturally it drapes his shoulders,
like a fine cloak tailored to fit.

I pause for a moment,
considering my own hunched stature.

I can't help but wonder
how it might feel
to stand so tall,
to boast so boldly,
to feel so at ease
in your own skin.

To believe in oneself
so fully.

As though admonishing me
for such insolence,
the sky darkens.

Somewhere deep within the woods,
a nightbird awakens; its shrill cry
sends a shiver down my spine.

This way, I say.
Mother asked us to fetch colocynth seeds.
Make haste. Dusk is nearly upon us.

Perhaps there are some in that tree! Photis trills,
extending his arms like wings,
pretending to fly
as he runs past me
toward a towering elm.
You said the best ones are up high!

I duck beneath a curtain of leaves,
cobwebs tangling in my hair.
The plant we seek grows on the ground, silly.

Perhaps I should just check the tree, he replies stubbornly.
Perhaps you should teach me to climb
so that I can help you look up there.
He gestures to the crooked limbs
looming large overhead
like the outstretched arms of a giant.

The sun dips lower,
the last of its yellow yolk
slipping beyond the horizon.

Not today, brother.
There is not enough light.

I am the light! he pronounces,
puffing his chest, making a joke
of his name.

Very clever, I reply,
cuffing his ears playfully.
One day, I will teach you to climb.

When? he whines.

Soon, I promise.

I lead him away from the elm
and toward a shallow trough
where a faint splash of color
has caught my eye.

You always say that, he sulks,
following me reluctantly.

Oh! Look, Photis!
I point to the ground,
hoping to distract him.
*You've stumbled straight into
a patch of colocynth! Well done!*

Near his feet, a fist-sized gourd lies among the leaves,
its hard skin mottled with green stripes.
Photis twists it from the vine,
cups the bitter fruit in his palms questioningly.

Mother will powder the pulp, I explain.
She will grind the seeds, pickle the rind.

She will waste nothing.
When I tell her you found this,
she will be very pleased.

He beams and places the gourd
in my basket, his tender pride
restored.

41.

Weeks pass.
The moon shrinks
smaller
and smaller
until it is nothing
but a silver sliver
ready to slice open
the dark sky,
reborn anew.

My gut wrenches
with a dull pain.
The small of my back aches.
I roll to my side in bed,
clutching my abdomen.

The sticky warmth of blood
smears my thighs.

I am startled at first, but
I am not afraid to bleed.
My mother prepared me for this.

She predicted it would happen
before my next birthday,
this synchronization of body and moon.

She is not angry
when I wake her.

I fill a bucket with water
and scrub the menstrual blood
from my sheets.
I rinse the red away,
pulling color from cloth,
which strikes me
as a strange reversal
of Father's work.

By candlelight,
Mother brews me a special tea
to mollify the cramping.

Transformation is often painful, Arachne.
But there is power to be found
in your new form.

I have never felt particularly powerful,
but I am hopeful that she is right.

෴

Over a steaming mug of tea,
we talk quietly
of growth and change
and womanhood.

I tell my mother
of the attention
Celandine attracts
when we are in public.

She exhales
a long breath.

Men often regard beauty
as an invitation,
as something
to possess,
to overtake,
to spoil.

I nod, for I have seen
the wolfish hunger
in their eyes.

I have felt their hands
tear a part of me
away, stealing me
from myself.
A part I worry
I may never reclaim.

Mother regards the faint scar on my face
where a branch scraped me once
while I climbed, years ago.

She runs her thumb along my cheek,
like she used to do when I was small,
when I was upset and needed to feel loved.

She studies me, as if she can read
my thoughts, sensing
deeper scars
beneath the surface of my skin.

Perhaps it is time
for some new stories, she says,
as though the tales she spins
are as potent as the herbs and roots
she blends into curing balms and soothing teas.
I am beginning to understand
that they are.

I curl close to her,
listening carefully,
grateful she has not
pushed me to share
a story of my own.

Knot

A story, told by Mother:

Helios deceives Leucothoe by disguising himself as her mother.
Imagine the sun god coming to you, my daughter, in my form.
Would you trust me? Of course you would.
You would have no reason to be afraid.
So trust is what Leucothoe does too.

She dismisses her attendants and servants.
She and Helios are now alone.
Unable to hide his passion any longer,
he reveals his true identity. Leucothoe shudders.
She knows instantly what he intends.

Men carry swords on their hips, and between their legs.
When they feel like it, they will use both to cut us down.
I do not tell you this to scare you, my child.
I only wish to arm you with truth.

In her fright, Leucothoe drops her distaff and spindle to the floor.
You see, she is a spinner, like you and me.

When the bards sing this next part, they choose
lyrical, unthreatening phrases like,

"dread makes her lovely,"
"her fright was most becoming,"
or "the fair maiden swoons."

But make no mistake: she is terrified.
There is an uninvited man—no, god—in her private chambers.
She asks him to leave. She tells him no. She tries to flee.

The sun god, undeterred, radiates so fiercely
that he blinds Leucothoe.
She cries out. She cannot see the doors or windows to escape.

Now, the bards will say that she is
               "defeated by the brightness of the god"
that she eventually
               "quits her protest"
then finally
               "endures his force"
or, worse,
               "takes his passion without complaint."

This is a gilded lie. Helios rapes Leucothoe.
His touch leaves her burned and blistered.

When you hear these stories, my child, do not pass lightly
over the silken prose, the lilting verse. Peel back the veneer.
Gaze upon the ugly truth beneath without fear.
Make yourself stronger with its knowing.

42.

When Celandine visits next
I plan to tell her my lunar cycle has begun.
I will tell her about Leucothoe, too,
so that we may wear these stories
like armor, together.

But when she appears,
positively beaming
in the midday light,
she is not alone.

A boy, Lykos, is by her side.
I recognize him from the market,
though he has never been cruel
like the others.
He is the metalsmith's son,
from a good, wealthy family.

Come, Arachne, Celandine says.
*Lykos says the green plums
have finally turned gold.
He found a wild grove.*

I squint at Lykos. He smiles back.
Two years older than me,
he is more man than boy,
barrel-chested, strapping,
charming even.

Helios shines warmly for us today, he says.
I bristle at the mention of that god,
especially after Mother's recent tale.

A cool breeze ruffles his dark hair.
Boreas sends the gift of wind, he adds.
We would be glad for your company, Arachne.

Won't you join us? Celandine adds.

We? Us? The coupling
of such small words
stings.

I avert my eyes and look instead
at the unfinished weaving waiting
upon my loom. I promised Mother
I would complete it today. I do not like
to break a promise. I do not like
to be apart from my friend, either.

Yet I cannot stop Celandine
from going with Lykos,
if that is what she wishes.

Perhaps another time, I say.

Celandine nods
then gazes at Lykos,
her eyes sparkling.

Very well, dear friend.
Return to your work, if you must.
We will bring you some plums.

43.

All day I regret
my choice to stay indoors,
instead of enjoying the sun
with Celandine and Lykos.
I am sullen and moody.

When Father enters the house,
he eyes the cloth
I wove earlier,
now draped over a chair
beside the loom.

He scowls, but that is
his neutral expression,
the result of long days
bent over a steaming vat
of putrid snails.

I chop vegetables
at the kitchen table,
while Mother finishes
a batch of herbal salves.

You made this, wife? Father says,
lifting the cloth to the light,
inspecting the weave.

No. It is your daughter's work, she replies.

Arachne?

My stomach twists.

Have you other daughters? Mother teases.

Father quirks an eyebrow.
He studies the cloth again.

I lower my chin, my nerves abuzz.

It is not bad, he says.

I look up, shocked.
My father is not an unkind person,
though he is stoic and stern,
rarely effusive with love or praise,
especially toward me.

Not bad at all.

This may be
the closest thing
to a compliment
he has ever paid me.

Indeed, Mother murmurs,
a faint smile tugging
the corners of her lips.

My heart batters my ribs.

Photis plays in the corner of the room,
oblivious to our conversation,

too busy crashing
his carved wooden soldier
against his wooden swan.

Will you bring it to the tradesmen
down by the pier? Mother asks, shocking me further.

I had assumed the cloth would be used
for kitchen rags, or loincloths.
It is hard to imagine
that my work might be destined
for something greater
than undergarments.

I will see if it may fetch some coins, Father says,
folding the cloth into a neat square.

He nods at me then
and when our eyes meet
I sense that, finally,
after all these years under the same roof,
he sees me.

⁓

Later that night,
sleep evades me.
I toss and turn
in my bed.
I feel as though
a sort of power hums
within the marrow
of my bones.

I do not know
what to do with this
unfamiliar sensation.
All I know
is that I want to
hold tightly to it.

44.

Overnight, that humming sensation
collects into a hard, tight knot
lodged within the center of my chest.

It glows, grows, growls.
A single cinder hungering for air,
waiting to spark and spread
like wildfire.

I awake uneasy and feverish.

I run to the riverbank
and splash water on my face,
watching as my unbeautiful features
rearrange themselves
in the river's glassy surface.

The villagers' voices
rise like mist around me:
            Such a sorry scrap of a girl . . .
                        No future, that one . . .

Tendrils of self-doubt and shame
emerge from the mud and muck,
writhing and twisting.

Invasive vines constrict
the nascent ember of pride
I cradle within me, strangling
its blasphemous brightness.

The vines thicken to thorny ropes.
They tighten around my limbs, my neck,
whispering, hissing.
      A girl like you is nothing . . .
           Nothing nothing nothing . . .

My ears ring, my vision warps.
The wind carries a distant song,
lutes screeching offkey, the bards singing
of hubris and hamartia.
      Beware beware beware . . .

I claw at my clothes,
desperate to free myself.

Naked, I plunge my body
into the river.
The cold is shocking,
cleansing.

I let the current
carry me
far away.

Then I dive
deep beneath
the surface
until I can no longer
hear any voice
but my own.

45.

Wool becomes thread,
thread becomes cloth,
cloth becomes coins,
coins become bread.

While Mother perfects her healing pharmaka,
blending and bending herbs and roots to her will,
I keep busy transforming wool into bread,
reveling in this simple magic.

Ever since I emerged from the river
I carry myself differently.

My knees remain crooked,
my gait is still ungraceful,
yet each step contains new energy.
Purpose propels me forward.

Even Celandine has noticed the change,
though she thinks it's because some boy
has captured my interest, which could not be
further from the truth.

I tear a chunk from the crusty loaf on the table.
I dip it into a shallow bowl of broth.

I chew thoughtfully,
savoring the nuttiness of the grains.

I gaze at the loom.
With more practice, I wonder
what else I may be capable of.

Movement catches my eye.

I spot a black spider suspended
between the rafters in our kitchen,
a fly ensnared in her web.

Her curved legs move furiously,
wrapping her prey in silk
like a miniature spindle.

When the work is done,
she feasts.

You and me, I say between bites of bread,
we are not so different.

46.

Have you ever seen the Minotaur? Photis asks
one afternoon in the garden.

He helped me weed for a while,
plucking each unwelcome sprout

with thunderous laughter
and a dramatic squeal,
playing pretend—a ruthless god
snatching up unsuspecting victims.

But the fun quickly wore off.
Now he sits on the fence post,
asking an endless stream of questions
while I toil in the midday heat.

I would much rather be inside,
weaving in the cool shade,
but I have already neglected
the vegetables for too long.

I have never seen the Minotaur.
Nor do I wish to, I say,
taking a swill of water
from a nearby jug.

His real name was Asterion.
Did you know that?

Photis shakes his head,
swings his legs.
Have you ever seen a bear?

Yes. Two, in fact.

Two! Where?
In the woods?
He hops off the fence, eyes wide,

his imagination captured
by the slightest whiff of adventure.

No, in the sky.

A flying bear?
A bear with wings?
Like the Pegasus?

Not quite. I laugh.
These bears are made of stars.

Stars? His brow furrows dearly.

I will show you one day
when the night sky is clear.
Callisto and Arcas,
mother and son.

He considers this for a moment.
Perhaps he has heard
some version of the tale.

Will Mother and I
become stars one day? Photis asks.

His question knocks the breath from me.
Not for a very long time, I reply.

I rise from the vegetable patch
and catch him in my arms,

mussing his dark hair.
He smells of fresh earth and sweet honey.

Unless you anger the god of weeding,
then who knows, I tease.
Best to help your sister
with her chores!

God of weeding?
There's no such thing!
He squirms and giggles
until I set him free.

47.

A half-moon later,
Father presents me
with several skeins
of sumptuous fiber.

I look down at the wool and flax,
soft-spun and saturated with color.
I am enamored with the material,
my fingers long to touch it,
but I worry I will mar the thread.
I fear I am not worthy
of such beauty.

Father squints at me, perplexed
by my hesitation.
He nudges the basket closer.

I look into his eyes, probing his face
for something. Permission, maybe?

He tips his chin,
his dark brown eyes softening.

Weave it well, daughter, he says
in his work-hardened way.

Unlike Mother, who regales me
with a steady stream
of stories and sage advice,
my father has never been
one for words.

He does not pat me on the back
like he does with Photis,
but this simple gesture
says enough.

His quiet trust in me
bellows the hollow cavity
within my chest,
kindling the ember lodged within,
stoking my determination
like the hungry fire Mother tends
beneath her boiling pot.

48.

The tapestry takes weeks.
Celandine and Photis
grow annoyed with me,

for I am hardly any fun, always
working, working. No time
for frolicking, or fruit picking,
or sword fighting with sticks.

I am torn, but I have little choice.
Father paid a large sum
to buy these yarns
and I feel tremendous pressure
to produce something worthy
of their price. Besides, I enjoy
this work. I like having
something that is mine,
something I may actually
be good at. Something
that helps feed
my spirit, and also
the people I love.

⚬⚭⚬

I choose for my subject
the meadow beyond our home,
stitching in tiny details—
  the curl of fiddleheads,
  yellow-throated crocus,
  bees and butterflies—
which help bring the scene to life.

Mother does not meddle
unless I seek her counsel.

When the tapestry is complete,

she presses her hands to her breast,
declares it beautiful.

Father regards the tapestry
with an unreadable expression.
Perhaps he envisioned something more exciting,
like a battle or chariot race.

But I have never been to battle,
nor have I witnessed a race.
For now, I weave what I know.

He rolls the tapestry carefully
to bring to the tradesmen.

It is hard to part
with my best work yet,
but we cannot afford
to keep it.

49.

After the sale of the tapestry,
we feast on lamb stewed with olives.

For this, we thank Arachne,
Mother says, looking at me
across the table.

Father and Photis
merely grunt in agreement,
their mouths too busy chewing.

I cannot tell
if it is the rich food,
the cup of wine,
or merely pride
that warms and
fills me so thoroughly.

If I could,
I would weave this moment
into a tapestry
to preserve forever.

50.

When I see Celandine next,
I give her a small pouch of almonds
bought with extra coins
from the sale of the tapestry.

Please don't be cross with me, I say,
worried she thinks I have chosen
work over our friendship
these last few weeks.

Cross? How could I be? she says,
popping an almond into her mouth.
Especially when you bring me these.

She smiles, but something in her face
looks different.
When I press her, she grows quiet.

Have you begun to bleed too? I ask.
It is perfectly natural. There is no shame in it.

She pales and runs away,
scattering almonds in the grass
as she leaves.

෴

I return to our house
confused and burdened
with remorse,
wishing I had not
upset Celandine,
replaying words
in my head,
wondering how
to make this right.

I look for Photis.
His raucous laughter
and bright spirit
are exactly what I need
to lift my mood.

Plus, he always knows
how to make Celandine smile;
perhaps he will give me
some useful advice.

On my way across the meadow
I find two hefty sticks—
perfect make-believe swords.

I will challenge Photis
to a duel along the riverbed.

Perhaps I will even
let him win this once.

I smile and set out
in search of my brother.

51.

A memory, raw and stinging,
like plunging an open wound into seawater:

Sickle-beaked crows
circle,
iridescent black wings
carve
gray marbled sky.

The air is oddly still.

I approach the oak tree,
calling out for Photis.

The crows scatter,
cawing insidiously
as they depart.

I look down.
The sticks fall from my hands.
My vision unravels . . .

                    hard-packed earth
            rough roots
                            jagged stone
                                    red blood
                    pooling
congealing
                    morbid halo
my brother's head
                        skull cracked
                            shock frozen
                                    unseeing eyes
            frighteningly wide

                                        broken branch
                                            clenched
                        rigid grip   small hand
            black-winged birds
        clotted clouds

                                        life spinning
                                                to a stop.

52.

Tears stain
my face
I tear
across
the field
running
screaming
until the
breath
runs out

Mother
frantic
drying
wet hands
on dry cloth
> *What is it, child?*
> *What is the matter?*
My mouth
gapes
dry sobs
caught
my throat constricting
heart imploding
chest compressing
I grip her
hand
run
pull her
toward
the base
of the tree
where
Photis
lies
dead.

53.

No, no, no! she howls.
My brother's blood
coats her fingers,
seeping deep

into the fabric
of her dress
as she cradles
his splintered skull,
his limp body,
in her trembling arms.

The moly! I croak,
when I can finally
breathe and speak again,
recalling the strange herb
we harvested long ago.
Can you use it?
Could it save him?

It is too late for that.
Once the soul has departed . . .
She hugs him close,
this sweet broken boy,
beloved brother,
treasured son
bright as the sun
after which he was named.

No! I protest, desperate,
devastated.
We have to try, I shriek.
There must be something!

It is too late, she repeats,
her voice hoarse.
He is gone.

I sink to the ground,
too stunned for tears.

My mother hangs her head
and weeps.

The rolling hills
fill with the sound.
Sorrow echoes
deep and low
like thunder.

54.

Soot-colored storm clouds
settle over our home.

When Photis dies
he takes with him
all the light.

Our life is dark now,
dim and wonderless.

I do not know
how we will survive
his death.

55.

Celandine brings us
boiled eggs and beans.

Her family is numerous and poor;
they have a dozen mouths to feed
and nothing to spare,
yet they give so much.

Her mother knows the pain
of a child, lost. It is not uncommon,
but that does not dull
the twisting knife of grief.

I am too racked with sadness
to remember why
Celandine and I quarreled
only days ago.

I thank her profusely for the food,
for her family's generosity.
Whatever mistakes I made
are forgotten, our friendship
restored.

She embraces me
and we cry together,
for she loved Photis too.

❧

Father retreats to the shore.
He claims to work longer and longer
at the dye vats, yet he brings home
less and less money.

When he does return,
his hands barely smell of fish.

It is clear the only thing he has dyed
is his beard, stained red with tavern wine.

56.

I drown too.
Not in wine
but guilt.

> *Will you teach me to climb?*

How many times
did Photis ask me this?

How many times
did I defer?

I failed him,
of this I am sure.

No, Celandine assures me
while we walk
through the pear orchard.

You did not fail him.
It was an accident.

An accident
that could have been

avoided, if only
I had taught him
to test the limbs
before setting his weight
fully upon them,
to beware of rotten branches,
to plan his descent
as carefully as his ascent.

If only
I had woven a great net
to hang beneath the boughs
to catch him, to keep him safe.
That is what a good sister would do.

I berate myself,
prostrate myself.

My mind spirals,
lost within a labyrinth
of loathing.

Arachne, please.
Celandine cups my face
in her palms.

She lifts my chin,
so that the sun falls
in warm slashes
across my cheeks,
reminding me
that Photis may be gone
but there is light left still.

You are not to blame.
Despite the sun's warmth,
I shiver.

If I am not to blame
then who, or *what*, is?

57.

I drag the axe,
its heavy blade
gouging the softened earth,
leaving deep, rutted scars
in my wake.

I cross the pasture,
heave the tool over my shoulder
and charge the mighty oak,
a warrior in battle.

I scream and hack and chop
until calluses tear open
across my palms.

My shoulders grow stiff,
my muscles ache in protest.
Wood chips and splintered bark
fall in great piles at my feet.

No matter how many times
I bring down the blade,
I cannot shear away

the regret, the rage
that entombs me.

I snap every branch I can reach.

I will build a pyre
with your limbs! I shriek,
like Minos unleashing his fury,
issuing empty threats
after Theseus's defeat of Crete.

I will reduce you
to nothing more
than a stump,
and then I will dance
atop your severed torso!

I bawl and bluster.
The oak tree stands
injured but indifferent,
unmoved, unbothered
by the pleas and pains
of a lowly mortal.

I choke back a sob,
blink back
the sting of tears.

I stare at the tree,
at the light filtering
through its emerald canopy.
Its leaves rustle in the breeze.

I smell the woody tang
of clear sap seeping
from its wounded middle.

My senses return,
my red-tinted wrath dulling
with each ragged breath.

With piercing clarity
I now see
that I am not avenging
my brother's death;
I am only hurting something
I once loved.

> *Felling one living thing*
> *will not bring back another.*
> I am sure I heard this
> in a story, once.

I drop the axe,
sink to my knees,
collapse against
the thick trunk
and beg forgiveness.

58.

I curse myself
for damaging
my most useful tool—
not the axe,
but my hands.

How will I weave or weed
or cook or sew
with such mangled paws?

Back at home,
I clean my palms well,
wincing as the water
washes over the blistered skin
like liquid flames.

Mother is asleep
so I help myself
to one of her salves.

I scoop and smear
a pine-scented balm
onto my torn hands,
hoping the mysteries
of Mother's pharmaka
will stave off festering sores
and numb the throbbing pain.

⟋⟍

I deliver a large bundle of kindling
to Celandine's family as a small token
of thanks for their recent generosity.

Her mother is grateful.
Just in time for baking, she says,
stacking the sticks neatly beside the hearth,
then feeding them, one by one,
into the oven's gaping maw.

Celandine eyes the vast pile of oak wood
and the bandages wrapping my hands.

Your temper burns hot, she says knowingly,
a warning note in her voice.

Not as hot as the fire
your mother builds, I reply.
Think of the crusty loaves that will rise
thanks to the fruits of my fury.

Celandine gives me a look.
Come, it is stifling inside.
Let us cool off
with a walk along the shore.

59.

Celandine and I stroll
side by side, our shoulders
bumping together easily.

I miss Photis deeply,
but with each step
along the water's edge
the incandescence of my anger fades.

Grief is harder to shake,
ebbing and flowing
like the tides themselves,
receding for stretches of time
before cresting and crashing once more,
        often without warning,

threatening to wreck me
against the jagged rocks
of remorse.

Still, the sea is a healing place;
I am glad Celandine brought me here.

I vow to return
if my temper flares again.
I cannot let it consume me
like it did earlier.

I cannot allow Aite—
goddess of ruin—
to whisper in my ear,
and spur me to destruction.

We walk far from the dye vats,
the ships, the piers,
until we are alone.

The sand shifts
beneath our bare feet.
The frothy surf
crashes, laps, licks
at our ankles.

The sea air entwines itself in our hair,
mine dark and stringy,
Celandine's soft and golden.

When I drag my tongue across my lips,
I taste salt upon them.

See how much cooler it is down here?
Away from that infernal kitchen, Celandine says,
splashing me playfully, the hem of her skirt
damp against her slender calves.

I nod. The breeze is crisp,
the water cold and refreshing.

Despite this, each time
Celandine's fingertips drift
toward my own
a shock of heat
courses through them.

I worry an infection smolders
beneath the bandages.
I unwrap the layers of gauze.

Miraculously,
my hands are nearly healed,
the skin pink and new.
Mother's salve has worked better
and faster than I expected.

If only one of her cures
could have revived Photis . . .

Another wave of grief.

I press my palms to my eyes
to stop a deluge of tears,
to quell the mounting anger.

If Mother could have saved him,
she would have.
If the moly or any other herb
could have helped him,
she would have used it.
Nothing would have stopped her.

I know this
with every part of my being.
Yet it does not prevent me
from wishing I could unwind
the spindle of time
and change everything.

Celandine pulls my hands
from my face.

Her eyes are liquid green,
the color of seawater captured
in shallow pools.

It's all right, she tells me,
clasping my hands in her own.
You will be all right.

In that moment
I choose to believe her.

Long after we depart the shore
warmth lingers in my hands,
tracing its way

from my fingertips,
up my arms,
into my chest,
and downward.

Even when I return home
a feverish flush lingers,
though I am not ill.

60.

That night
I dream of the sea,
of oak branches
tumbled in the surf
whittled and smoothed
into driftwood
curving and gray,
dancing ankles
frilled with white froth.
I dream of flotsam
and feathers
and softly lapping waves.
I dream of Celandine,
of pyres and palms,
of salt-kissed lips.
Of fires
that an entire ocean
cannot douse.
Of a thirst
that water
cannot quench.

61.

Mourning withers Mother.
She sits by the window,
a dry husk
of her former self,
turning Photis's wooden toys
over and over
in her palms.

I mine my memories
for a story, a balm
of spoken words, to heal
or at least soothe her.

I choose a tale from childhood
that Photis and I both loved,
about Orpheus's golden harp
and its ability to make animals,
trees, even rocks dance to its tune.

I recite every line,
recall each charming detail,
adding flourishes here and there.
I let my voice rise and fall,
mimicking the bard's merry melody.

I even gesture with my fingers,
pretending to play our loom's strings
like an instrument
to bring the story to life.

When I finish,
my mother looks at me
with vacant eyes,
as though I have told
the entire tale
in a tongue
she does not
understand.

⟨⟩

I drag the loom before my mother
and encourage her to weave.
This, I know, is a language
she speaks fluently.

Mother stares at the warp.
She places Photis's toys
on the windowsill.

I balance the loom weights
and adjust the frame.
The wood whines and resists
as though it mourns too.

Mother takes a deep breath,
traces the threads
with her fingertips,
like a harpist strumming
a silent song.

Encouraged,
I leave to milk the goat

and tend the garden
before weeds suffocate it
completely.

When I return,
Mother is curled in her cot.
I look at the loom.
She has snipped every thread.

62.

I plead with Mother to rise,
to collect herbs,
to grind the pestle,
to return to her life,
      for she is lucky to have it.

She has me, too,
I remind her gently,
squeezing her shoulder.

Mother once said
that the key to pharmaka
is learning to bend the world
to your will.

But when you lose your will,
what can you do?

I fear something
deep within her
is damaged.

I fear she is
coming apart
at the seams.

If I had any calluses left,
I would chew them
from my fingers, fretting.

I can repair the loom's warp.
I can re-knot each severed string.

But I do not know
how to mend
a broken heart.

63.

I wander the moonlit woods
searching for wild herbs,
for something to cure
my mother's spirit.

But the rocky ground
does not offer up
any secrets to me.

In the shadowed distance
a wisp of movement
catches my eye.

A nymph enrobed in sheer linen
slips ghostlike

between temple columns,
where tendrils of white smoke rise.

I have not seen a nymph in these parts
for many years. I pause to watch her.

I wonder if she belongs
to Athena's retinue.

From the bards' songs and Mother's tales,
I know that some gods travel with an entourage
of these elusive and alluring maidens,
minor deities of moss and mountain,
spring and stream.

The nymph winds between the temple columns,
her body lithe, her movement languid.

My pulse quickens.
I feel an urge to follow her,
but I stop after a few steps,
remembering that only cavernous silence
and cold indifference await
within the temple walls.

Behind me, a twig snaps.
I startle, turn my head.

Celandine stands, nymphlike
in the glowing moonlight
her face clouded with questions.

I saw you from my window, Arachne.
What are you doing out so late? she asks,
rubbing her arms to keep warm.
It is too cold to sleep on the knoll
and watch the stars.

I hold up my empty basket.
I shake my head miserably.

Time, she says softly, understanding.
She needs time to heal, Arachne.
No herb nor root will do.

64.

Days hobble ahead.
Father is nowhere
to be found.

Mother is numb
and immobile.

We cannot accept
any more charity
from Celandine's family.

If we are to eat,
it will be thanks
to me.

The skin on my palms
is still tender

but my hands
are healed enough
to weave.

In time, I will earn
new calluses.
My skin will toughen
and thicken again.

In time—like Celandine says—
my heart will heal too.
As will Mother's, I hope.

I gather all the yarn I can find
and set to work.

The boxwood shuttle
feels foreign at first,
but slowly we become
reacquainted.

A day passes,
then two.
Spin, weave, sweat, sleep.

Finally, a bolt of cloth
emerges.

And just in time;
our cupboard is nearly bare,
my hip and collarbones
jutting dangerously.

When I am done weaving,
I set off to trade my finished fabric
for food and wool in Hyponia.

I am weak and exhausted
and I do not like walking to town alone,
but Celandine is busy
caring for her younger sisters
so she cannot accompany me today.

I gird myself,
fending off memories
of the boys on the winter road.

I fill my pockets with rocks
in case I need something to throw.

65.

I arrive safely and make my way
toward the market stalls.

It is noisy and crowded,
the air thick with the stench
of animals and rotting fruit.

I am not skilled at haggling.
I do not have a head for numbers
and I find it hard to put a price
on the fabrics I have made.

Negotiating is a game
I have not yet learned to play.

My nerves rattled,
my stomach growling,
I sell my wares hastily,
surely for less than they are worth,
a choice I instantly regret.

I hurry away, shame trailing me
like a hungry dog hoping for scraps.

I dislike the way
the vendors stare
and whisper
behind their hands
when they see me pass.

I am tired, starving, and raw,
my temper hot as coal.

I snap at them and shout,
What do you want?
Leave me be!

You are the daughter of Idmon?

I pause. *Yes.*

Has something happened to Father?
Has he stumbled off the pier,
drunk on wine and grief?

Was it you, girl, who wove the tapestry?
That he traded some months ago?

A very fine one—an idyll
of butterflies and flowers.

I nod, my face ablaze.

Their words surprise me.
I had thought they judged me
for my homely features, my odd gait,
my poor negotiation skills.
But it seems . . . they praise me?

Their attention
unnerves me.

Make another! someone calls out.

Rumor has it
the satrap's wife desires a new tapestry
to hang in the palace.

A commission of that caliber
is unfathomable. Besides,
I do not seek fame,
only bread and cheese
to feed my family.

Surely, they mock me.
Color creeps up my neck.

I grab my basket
and run, stopping only
when my feet reach the sea.

66.

I sink into the sand,
breathing hard.

I am blessedly alone
on an ivory stretch of beach,
save for a few seabirds.

They dip and wheel in the air,
crashing into white-tipped waves
like spears, drawing fish from the water
to feed openmouthed chicks
nestled high in stony bluffs.

I exhale and stretch my knees,
which ache from running.

In the distance, a ship glides toward the pier,
its hundred oars like the legs of a centipede.

I lose track of time
sitting on that beach,
listening to the waves.

Only when a gull screeches,
cracking a clam
onto the rocks nearby,
do I become aware
that the sun is shining.

The somber clouds
that have persisted
for weeks finally clear.

A pearlescent shell
shaped like a fan
shimmers in the sand
by my feet.

I pick it up, slip it
into my pocket.

67.

I arrive at home
with a calm spirit
and sea air entangled
in my hair.

I place the shell
next to my mother's bed.

She opens her eyes.
Where have you been, Arachne?

I am pleased she noticed my absence.
Down at the beach.
And the market.

She sits up.
I think I would like to go there.

Her voice is raspy with disuse
but I hear the faintest glint
of light in her tone.

The market? I ask.

No, the sea.

My heart swells,
crashing like a wave,
relieved to see her
coming back to life.

68.

We visit the ocean together.

Each morning
before the day's work begins
we climb atop a rocky outlook,
to watch as the dawn sun
burns away the evening mist,
feeling our own sorrow
slowly dissipate with it.

Standing beside her, I rest my head
upon my mother's shoulder,
for I am as tall as her now,
my body more woman than girl.

With our feet rooted to stone,
and Mother's arm around my waist,
I feel grounded, even when
the sea wind howls, threatening
to knock us off our perch.

69.

We gradually return
to our daily rhythms,
stepping carefully around
our loss, as though
the abyss of absence
is a forbidden well.

We learn to avoid
its crumbling, unstable edges
for fear of stumbling, plunging
into its limitless depths.

We do our best to honor Photis
in our own small ways
but we do not reopen the wounds
that are still so tender.

Father is scarce,
but when he does return home
he brings bags of colored fleece,
which I card and spin and weave.

He wordlessly exchanges
each length of finished cloth
for sacks of grain and other goods.

Between wool and wheat,
my hands are in constant motion,
working, weaving, kneading,
repeating
until our cupboard shelves

are no longer bare
and the jagged angles
of my protruding hip bones
soften into smoother lines.

⌀

Mother begins to reclaim
the garden, to ready the soil
for next year's crops.

She rakes out winter's detritus,
clears away ossified stalks,
tames unruly brambles.

Each seed she plants
carries the promise
of tomorrow.

I feel new hope grow
for the first time
in months.

70.

One clear night
Celandine raps my sill
with her knuckles.

Come, she whispers.
*The sky is too beautiful
to ignore.*

You are too beautiful to ignore, I reply, half-asleep,
though there is truth in my words.

So say the village boys, she laughs,
then cups a hand over her mouth
to stifle the sound.

I slip from bed and join her,
a blanket rolled beneath my arm.

We lie upon the grassy knoll
and gaze at the stars.

She points to Andromeda,
then at Perseus, their love so true
it was sewn into the stars.

I become aware of the nearness
of our bodies. I want to draw myself
closer still, to close the gap between us,
to feel the warm press
of her skin on mine.

Then she speaks of Lykos.

I withdraw, the night air
suddenly colder than it was
only a moment before.

There is a giddiness
in Celandine's voice
as she whispers and giggles,

telling me about the doting boys
who vie for her attention.
One, it seems, has caught her eye.

When she imagines her Perseus—
               her own star-sewn love—
is it Lykos she sees in the sky beside her?

Long after she falls asleep,
I lie awake, acutely aware
of the distance
between us.

The stars wink
and spin and fade.

I spot the constellation of Callisto,
fair maid turned to bear.
> *When Zeus came to her full of lust,*
> *he disguised himself as Artemis.*
> *Unaware of the ruse,*
> *Callisto embraced the goddess,*
> *whom she trusted and adored.*
> *She swore her devotion to Artemis,*
> *placed kisses upon her mouth*
> *freely, passionately,*
> *not understanding until too late*
> *that deception and heartbreak lurked*
> *behind that tender embrace.*

I find no solace
in this tale tonight,
only heat and shame.

Flushed, frustrated,
I toss the blanket aside.
Restless, wrestling
with a tumult of emotions.

71.

Dawn breaks
splashing a garden of color—
       lavender, apricot, rose—
across the sky.

Birdsong warbles
from the treetops.
Dew collects
in heavy droplets
along silken webs.
The pigs in the sty
wake and snuffle.

I look over at Celandine,
sleeping peacefully.

I feel as though my chest
houses a hive.
A thousand bees hum
within my rib cage.
I don't know what to make
of this buzzing sensation
located so very close
to my heart.

The new day brings
light and life
but little clarity.

72.

Mother and I walk
along the beach.

She fills a basket
with seaweed and driftwood.
She wears her hair loose.
The wind whips it across her face.
She does not seem to mind.

She crouches to greet a scuttling crab,
its bulbous eyes unblinking,
its claw raised defensively.

Mother looks up at me and smiles.
I smile back.

While she continues to gather seaweed,
I gather my courage.

I want to speak with her
about the tangled emotions,
hopes, and desires
rising in me lately,
casting my thoughts
this way and that,

like an oarless boat
tossed upon ocean waves.

Perhaps she can guide me
to calmer waters.
Perhaps one of her stories
will offer the kernel of wisdom
my troubled soul seeks.

When I lift my chin to speak,
I see that she has moved
farther along the beach.

She dips a toe into the surf.
She laughs and wades
up to her ankles,
and then to her knees,
in the brisk salt water.

Come out from there, I scold
as though I am the mother
and she, the reckless child.
*It may be spring
but it is still too cold to swim.*

The wind steals my words,
or perhaps
she ignores me.

Either way, she stays too long
in the frigid sea.

73.

I notice the ruddiness
of her cheeks
as we arrive home
in the late afternoon.

It is just the healthy glow
of fresh air and a long walk, she insists.

But by midnight
a fierce chill
seeps into her bones.

She shakes and sweats
with fever.

I find our thickest blanket
and wrap her in its warmth.

I boil water for tea.
I wipe her brow
with a damp cloth.

I search the cupboard
and carry an armful
of tonics and salves
to her bedside.

Which one would help? I ask.
Unlike spinning and weaving,
I have never understood
the intricate workings
of Mother's pharmaka.

She points to a curved clay pot.
I spread the balm on her chest,
its aroma rich and herbal.

Next, I spoon a thick brown syrup
into her mouth. She grimaces
and asks for water to wash it down.
If it tastes as bad as it smells,
I do not blame her.

And this one? I ask,
holding up a small leather pouch
with a tear-shaped vial inside.

She shakes her head.
Put that aside for now.
And be careful with it, please.

I set the pouch on the table.
When I turn around,
she is fast asleep,
the fever at bay.

I cannot sleep
so I sit at the loom
and weave a shawl
of the softest wool
for my mother,
never imagining
it might become
a shroud.

74.

Arachne . . .
Daughter . . .

I wake disoriented,
dreaming that the wind
whispers my name
over and over.

Arachne . . .

I sit up. It is not the wind.
It is Mother.

I scramble out of bed
and rush to her side.

She shivers.
Her skin burns.

Daughter . . .
Her voice is as fragile
as the wings of a moth
beating faintly, circling
life's flickering flame.

A barking cough
rattles her chest.

I reach for the balm,
but she stops me.
Not that one.

She grasps the small leather pouch.
She removes the glass vial.

I see now that it is
attached to a length
of braided cord.

Shall I uncork it? I ask.

She shakes her head
before a fit of coughing
consumes her.

I lift a cup of water
to her mouth,
which she drinks
in sputtering sips.

When she recovers,
she whispers,
Lean close, my child.

She slips the braided cord
over my head
so that the tiny vial
hangs like a pendant
around my neck.

What is this?

She brushes a lock of hair
from my face.

There may come a time
when this world seems
too cruel, too unkind,
too unfair to bear.

But please, my child,
do not seek to depart.
Instead, weave for yourself
a better world, one worthy
of your gifts.

My eyes cloud with tears.
I . . . I . . . do not understand.
What do you mean?

The moly. She touches a finger
to the vial around my neck.
Its sap is contained inside.
When the time comes,
drink it
and make a wish.

A wish? Oh, Mother.
An herb cannot grant a wish.
The fever, it muddles your mind.
I press a cool compress
to her forehead.

Arachne, listen.
There is powerful magic
within this vial—within you.

No. This is absurd.
If she ever possessed real magic,
she would have used it
to revive Photis
when he fell
from the tree.
She would use it now
to heal herself.

Remember, new life begins
where another ends.

She taps the vial once more.
But be warned: this is a last resort.

Her eyelids flutter.
Her chest rises and falls.

Wait. Mother. Please—
I squeeze her hand.

Spin, my child, spin,
she murmurs as though she hears
some distant, dancing song.

Mother!

Her eyes flit open.
Her gaze lingers on my face,
weaving me
into her memory,

a tapestry, a portrait,
an image to last.

Her voice fades,
I love you so very much. . . .

She closes her eyes.
Her chest rises
then falls, rises
falls
and then
she is gone.

PART II

Unraveling

I do not remember
the year that follows
my mother's death.

I live in a haze
of tears
and weak broth.

Father comes and goes
like an apparition,
smelling of fish and wine,
wine and fish.

Grief cleaves
and wrenches
us apart,
shatters us
to pieces.

I cannot remember
if he embraces
or soothes me,
but this has never

been his way,
so I doubt it.

Like the snails
he crushes for dye,
he constructs
a carapace
around himself,
a hardened shell
into which
he disappears.

I cry so much
I wonder
if I might become
a river.

It happens sometimes,
according to the poets.

I dream fitfully,
nightmares, mostly.
Of mothers lost at sea,
bursting into flame.
Of brothers tumbling
from the sky.

I am haunted
by hallucinations
of transformation.

Of shedding
my skin.

Of becoming
a tree,
a bear,
a lark.

I envision
an escape
from this mortal life,
which feels
impossible to live.

Shadows gather
in the corners
of our home.

They sprout limbs
and claw at me
with dusky fingers.
I wake up
screaming.

⁓

Outside, the light
is so bright
it blinds me.

I shade my eyes
with my hands
and curse Helios.

I see two mounds
of earth in the field

beyond the garden:
        one big,
        one small,
        side by side.

Mother and Photis.

At least they are together.
At least they no longer suffer.

I do not remember
the burials.

I have no recollection
of weaving
the black wool cape
which drapes
my shoulders, heavy
as Sisyphus's stone,
day and night.

I pray,
but I know not
to whom.

I ache for solace,
for some shred
of faith or guidance.

Even in my darkest hour
no god or goddess

takes notice
of me.

᭶᭶

I find
a loaf of bread
on the table
and broth
in the pot.

Just enough
to keep me
alive.

Time hangs,
suspended,
spinning,
adrift.

I smell
lavender
and sea brine
which tells me
Celandine
has come
and gone.

She has cared for me
for days,
maybe months?
I do not know.

I know nothing.
I am nothing.
Soon I will
turn to ash.

Bitter
winter wind
carries me
to the sea,
turns me
to salt.

I wash ashore,
tumbled
like a rock,
whittled
like a grain
of sand,
so small
so . . .

Arachne! Arachne!
Celandine grips my shoulders.
She shakes me.
Enough!

Rewinding the Shuttle

1.

A fresh skein of wool, pale as cream,
hangs beside my loom.

I use it like a rope
to drag myself to shore,
for I was drowning.
Now I thrash and gasp for air.

The wool is an invitation, an ultimatum.

My eyes are sore in their sockets.
The wool is soft to the touch.

I am ancient and haggard.
I am newborn and unformed.

No! I shove the madness away.

I am fifteen. I have life in me yet.
I will not waste it.

I push the loom close
to our largest window
to take advantage
of the afternoon's golden light.

In the pasture
wildflowers bloom.

How brave they must be
to flourish
in this harsh, unkind world.

And yet, they do.

Their colorful petals
are an act of rebellion.

I breathe deeply,
watch deeply.

I had forgotten
how beautiful
the world could be.

Across the loom's barnacle-scarred beam
I stretch a line of thread, a lifeline,
a direct line to the memories
of my mother who taught me,
the grandmother who taught her,
and all the women who came before.

I wrap the shuttle with yarn,
pass it from palm to palm.

Tell me a story, the loom whispers,
speaking to me at long last.
Tell me your story.

I do not know which story to tell.
I still have so much of myself
yet to discover.

So, I retell the stories
given to me by my mother.
Seeking new meanings
and meager comforts
in the remembrance
of her voice and words.
Forging some sort
of rebellious beauty
out of the pain.

Knot

A story, continued:

When Leucothoe's father learns of her loss of virginity
at the hands of Helios, he is outraged and furious.
Not at the offending god, but at his daughter.

Leucothoe protests. "He raped me!" she cries,
pointing an accusatory finger
at the sun in the sky, guilty but untouchable.

Despite her honesty, her conviction, the charred flesh
and weeping burns that Helios's touch left across her body,
Leucothoe's father does not believe her.
He offers no pity nor comfort. What does he do instead?
He buries her alive.

Helios, in an unusual act
of overdue pity or performative remorse,
transforms Leucothoe into frankincense.
Strange, indeed. And impossibly unfair.

The innocent girl burns either way.

2.

Instead of soothing me
as I had hoped,
the remembered stories
bring anger to a seething boil.

My fury is a beast,
like Scylla in her rocky lair,
hungry, so hungry
for justice and revenge.

My fingers twitch.
This time, I leave the axe in the shed.
Instead, I reach for my shuttle.

I begin to weave
something new.

Leucothoe emerges,
her face and fear sewn
into the cloth,
vivid and arresting.

I stop myself
and step away
from the loom,
frightened
by the tapestry
I have created.

There is a reason
the villagers never hear
these stories—never *see* them—
not like *this*, parsed and peeled.
It is far too uncomfortable,
far easier to avert your eyes,
cover your ears.

Besides, the bards would never dare
to speak ill of the gods,
no matter how unjust or ugly
the truth may be,
for fear of retribution.
   A chill snakes down my spine.
   Perhaps I shouldn't, either.

I unstitch the weft, erase the image,
until the vertical warp hangs bare.

As soon as the undoing is complete
a deep ache settles in my chest,
a lingering sense of cowardice,
as though Leucothoe herself
is looking down on me,
her disappointment palpable.

The shuttle whispers—
not a soothing *husha-hush*,
but a disapproving *tsk-tsk*—
as I pass it back and forth,
weaving a new and neutral cloth.

3.

A few days later
Celandine invites me to join
a picnic with a group of friends—
        Demetria, Nereus, Arista, Lykos—
young village men and women of similar age
whom she has grown close with this past year
while I retreated into mourning.

They flit around her like butterflies.
I don't blame them; her warmth
and good nature are infectious.
Unlike me, Celandine has always been
affable and at ease with others.

Come with us, she implores,
leaning on the sill of my open window.
She lays her head on her folded hands.
Give that loom a rest, Arachne.

Lykos eyes my work.

*Perhaps you should try
a tighter weave along the edges?* he says,
his handsomely sculpted brow wrinkling.

My face reddens.
For a moment I think
        maybe he is right,
        maybe my work *is* flawed.

But this boy has never touched a loom.
His fingers are not embroidered with scars,
nor stained with errant dye, like mine.

I wish to correct him,
to explain why
the weave must remain loose
along these edges.
There is a strategy to it, an art.

And see this here?
He reaches through the window
and pokes the weft.
It could be finer.

I nearly slap his hand away.
The others laugh, all except Celandine,
who shoots him an annoyed look.

He knows nothing
of this craft
and yet—
and yet!
He feels no shame
speaking his mind,
offering unrequested,
unhelpful advice.

He puffs his chest
as though he has done me
some great service.

I wish to speak my mind too,
to cut him down
like a sapling
met with a sharpened axe.
But the words stick in my throat
and will not budge.

My cheeks are aflame,
which infuriates me more,
because when Lykos sees
the carmine color creeping
into my face,
he thinks I blush for him,
when in fact
I silently rage.

The sun is high.
Let us go, Arista says impatiently,
looping her elbow into Celandine's.

I feel an unexpected twinge of jealousy,
watching these girls link arms,
and it throws me even more
off balance.

Will you please come? Celandine asks,
as though reading my thoughts.

I shake my head. *Not today.*

Normally, I would be content
to see her skip gaily

in their midst,
to listen to her laughter.

But today I am unsettled
by the rush of emotions
that have risen
like an unexpected tide.

Enjoy yourself, I tell Celandine,
forcing false cheer
into my tone.

She departs with a sigh.
Halfway down the lane
she turns to look back.

Squint as I might,
I struggle to decipher
the look in her faraway eyes.

4.

I awake near midnight in a cold sweat,
certain someone is watching me.

The tips of my toes tingle.

I sit up.
The room is empty.

Father snores from his bed.
An owl hoots in the distance.

I must have been dreaming.

5.

In the morning,
something is awry.

The warp of my loom
has been altered
ever so slightly.

Under cover of nightfall,
someone added two rows of stitching
to my cream-colored cloth.

I think of Lykos's meddling words,
though surely it was not he
who did this. Boys are rarely taught
to spin and weave. Perhaps it was
one of the others, Arista or Demetria.
But why?

If this is meant as a message,
it is an undecipherable one.

How did they enter the house?
Why would they insert themselves
into my work this way?

When I tell Father, he asks
if I have been drinking his wine.

I think of Leucothoe's father,
who didn't believe her either.
Why are women's words
so easily dismissed?

I know the infraction is minor,
but I cannot help but feel violated.

I redo the stitches—fine as they may be—
reclaiming the work
as mine alone.

6.

Murmurs ripple
through the market:
      Athena was seen
      at her altar last night,
      gathering offerings.

She was displeased, a farmer says,
practically shaking.

Her ire caused a storm
that uprooted my cabbages!

Perhaps you should show her
more respect, an old woman grumbles,
pushing a cartload of gourds.

Respect? Please, woman.
Smoke rises from the temple day and night.
Her altars are never bare.

We can barely feed ourselves,
let alone leave fruit to rot
at her feet, murmurs the tanner,
careful not to speak too loudly.

My skin prickles.
I think of my loom, disrupted.
Could the goddess have visited *me* last night?

Impossible. My past prayers
were never answered.

I possess nothing worthy
of the gods' attention,
no divine or noble blood,
no great fortune or history to my name.
I have no reason to believe
Athena knows I exist at all.

I picture my loom once more,
the strangeness of foreign threads
interwoven with my own.

Then I shake my head,
dismiss the foolish idea,
and move on with my errands.

7.

The sky is cerulean,
daring me to attend

the spring festival
in the village square.

You shall have me go alone? Celandine pouts,
unfairly pretty even when she frowns.

We have both recently celebrated
our sixteenth birthdays,
but she has blossomed
in ways I have not.

What of your sisters? Or Lykos?
Will he not accompany you?

I suppose he will, she says,
twisting a lock of hair absentmindedly.
But it is your company I desire.

My heart quickens.
I avert my eyes, discomfited by the warmth
her words bring to my cheeks, my chest.

I tire of his attention, Arachne.

I do not blame you, I reply.

She laughs and pinches my arm.
Please come?

Soon. After I finish this cloth, I say, torn.
And then I will be free.
          At least until I must
          buy bread again. . . .

With Mother gone
and Father increasingly absent,
I must work harder than ever
in the garden and at the loom
if I wish to eat.

A cloud passes over the sun,
casting the room in shadow.

How long? She tugs at my sleeve.
Her fingertips graze my wrist.

Very soon. I promise.
I try to keep my voice steady
in spite of the stirring
I feel inside.
I will meet you there.

Celandine exhales. *All right.*

*Don't have too much fun
without me,* I call after her,
cursing the work I cannot ignore,
longing to walk beside her in the sunlight
and feel her fingertips
graze my wrist once more.

8.

I should have gone with Celandine.
I should have worked quicker.

I should have been there
when she needed me.

I was not.

Did I learn nothing
from the warnings
woven within
Mother's myths?

9.

I find Celandine weeping
in the tall grass
beyond our pasture.
In that same green place
where we first met
all those innocent years ago.

Her right eye is swollen shut,
the skin shiny and taut as a drum.

Who did this? I ask,
though I fear
I already know
the answer.

Lykos, she sobs,
wincing in pain.

She will never see
the world the same—

not just because
her eye is injured,
but because a carefree afternoon
ended with such abuse.

Her voice is brittle
as dried leaves.
There were three,
Lykos among them.

She lifts her sleeves and hem.
Color blossoms
in garish patches
across her neck,
wrists, and thighs,
where they choked her,
pinned her down, beat her
when she struggled.

The foretaste of vomit
rises in my throat.
Anger burns within my veins,
hot as molten bronze.

Do you believe me? she asks, trembling,
rearranging her dress.

Of course I believe you, I say, aghast.
How could I not?

He kissed me once before, you know?
A few days before Photis fell.

I had imagined as much.

I liked him well enough.
If I'm being truthful,
I wanted him to kiss me.

Though when he finally did,
he was rough and rude,
not sweet or gentle.

I did not like his tongue in my mouth.
It was slippery like an eel and revolting.

I did not want his body
pushed so close to mine.

But how could I tell him this?
It would have damaged his pride.

Besides, all the girls swoon when he is near.
Perhaps the problem was not him, but me?

She hangs her head.
I was too embarrassed
to tell anyone, even you.

I nod, knowing
exactly how that feels.

Lykos knew I was upset.
He apologized and I forgave him.

What else could I do?

I decided everything would be fine,
as long as we were not alone together.
He would not try to kiss me if others were near.

When he offered to walk me home
through the trail in the woods,
I declined. But then he said his friends
would accompany us. We would not be alone.

I felt safe . . . until I didn't.

She doesn't need
to tell the rest.
I do not ask for more.

I hold Celandine in my arms
and rock her like a child,
like she held me
in the numb blur of days
when I mourned
my mother and brother.

I should have gone with you, I say,
aching with remorse.

Perhaps I could have helped.
Maybe I could have stopped this.

I say the words
and there is a salve

to their saying,
but we both know
they are untrue.

Boys like Lykos
learn from the gods
to take what they want;
there is no stopping
the avarice of entitlement.

I gently clasp
her bloodied hands
in my own.
*I am so very angry
and so very sorry.*

10.

Celandine says
she fought so fiercely
against their advances,
that she slashed
Lykos's face
with her nails,
tearing a deep gouge
above his left eyebrow.

It will leave a scar, she says
with little satisfaction.

He will tell everyone
it was just a brawl

between the boys.
He may even wear it
like a badge of honor.

Celandine, on the other hand, will bear
much deeper scars, for as long as she lives.
Scars no one will ever see.

Except me. I see them.
I will not forget.

11.

I lie awake at night
roiling with rage,
racked with anguish.

If only Mother were still alive,
she would know what to do.

She would blend a sleeping draught
to help Celandine rest, a poultice
to soothe her bruises, a goose fat ointment
to rub into the folds of torn and tender skin.

And maybe even a poison
to slip into Lykos's wine.

The hair on my neck
stands on end.

I open my eyes
in the darkness

and realize
this is the first time
I have contemplated
murder.

I am surprised and unnerved
by how easily, how quickly
the thought presents itself,
as if some primal instinct
has been awakened.

12.

If not death, then surely some justice
must be served
for such a heinous crime.

I ask Celandine
if she will bring charges
against Lykos and the others.

She shakes her head.
None but I
will pay for this,
don't you see?

Before he left her
broken in the woods,
Lykos gave a warning:
>   *Keep your mouth shut.*
>   *You may use it*
>   *to sing pretty songs, or*
>   *to pleasure a man, or*

to praise the gods.
Otherwise,
keep your mouth shut.

He said his reputation
would be tarnished
if she speaks out.

His chance
at a bright future, dulled.

His family's good name, soiled.

While Celandine recounts the exchange,
my shock sours into disgust,
which ferments into fury.

To my mind,
the only thing
Lykos deserves
is to be castrated
like a bull.

Then he said,
if she dares to speak out—beware—
he will, too.

And his voice
will drown hers out.

Don't forget,
gossip spreads quicker
than hems gather mud.

Soon everyone will learn
what a shameful whore
pure, sweet Celandine really is.

13.

Even if Celandine swears
on her virtue, her innocence,
people will insist
that she brought this fate
upon herself.

They will click their tongues,
raise judgmental eyebrows.

The villagers will blame
  the sway of her hips,
  the drape of her dress,
  the blush of her cheeks.

They will blame
  her family,
  her friends,
  every choice she has ever made.

But why does no one
ever think to blame
  the boys?

They will say
teach your daughters
to be chaste and good.

Why not teach your sons
to be the same?

14.

How can I help? I ask, prepared
to go to battle like the woman warrior
Photis once claimed couldn't exist.

*All I want
is to escape this.
To disappear forever.*

Celandine, what are you saying?

I plan to run away, she tells me.

I cannot hide my surprise.

*Some place Lykos and the others
will never find me, or remind me
of what they've done,* she explains.
*Where the eyes of the village
cannot judge me for a crime
I did not commit.*

I think of Daphne—
the story Mother told me long ago—
of nymph turned to laurel tree.

Unable to run,
forced to endure
unwanted advances,

rooted in silence
for eternity.

I do not wish that same fate
for my friend, nor for anyone.
And yet, the thought of Celandine leaving
feels like a blade cleaving my heart in two.

I have a cousin in Colophon, Celandine continues.
She is a few years older, married, with a baby.
She has always shown me kindness.
I think she will take me in.

Colophon is quite far, I say, my voice weak,
overcome with fresh grief I try to keep at bay.

I only hope it is far enough.

I understand why she must leave, but—
I will miss you so much. . . .

You could come too, she says.
The city is famed
for its textile workshops.
I hear they seek weavers
and pay a good wage.
We could find work together.

My nearly cleaved heart
knits itself back together
as I consider her words.

There is so little left
for me here in Hyponia,
in this small village
and smaller house.
Mother and Photis are gone.
Father is scarce.

If Celandine departs too, then what?

Perhaps my future lies elsewhere.
In a sprawling city by the sea.
With my dearest friend by my side.
The prospect excites and terrifies me.

When do you plan to go? I ask.

In one week's time.
A caravan of wagons
is set to take miners to the quarries
a day's journey northeast of here.

I plan to hide among them
and dismount when they stop
on the northbound road,
which hugs the coast.

From there, it is two or three days' walk
to Colophon, unless I can find
transport aboard a cart or mule.

I am quiet, processing
everything she has said.

The plan sounds dangerous,
full of risks and uncertainties,
but when I look at her bruised face
I understand that fleeing
may be safer than staying.

What say you, Arachne?
She bites her swollen lip.
Do you think I am mad?

Not at all.
I think you are brave.

She nods, eyes brimming
with fresh tears. *And will you . . . ?*

Celandine doesn't even finish her question.

Yes, I tell her. *I will join you.*
And I will weave us both
a disguise.

I am startled by the speed at which
the words fly from my lips,
the decision made by my heart
before my head has time
to dissect or dissuade.

I can see in Celandine's face
that she needs me,
and that is reason enough.

If we are to face peril,
we shall do it together.

15.

One of my great woes
will be parting
with my loom.

Much of our journey
will be on foot;
even if I were to
disassemble the loom,
there is no way
I could carry
the heavy timbers
on my back.

I run my palms along
the time-smoothed frame,
stopping to admire
its circular sea-marks.

I think of the barnacles
that once clung
to a ship's underbelly,
the planks of which
were once a tree.

What a life
this wood has had.

I rub oil into
the loom's arthritic joints
until they cease
to whine and creak.

I adjust the weights, cupping
each pyramidal stone in my palm
until they hang just right,
pulling the strings taut,
keeping everything
in balance.

I pick up the shuttle,
whittled from boxwood
and oblong in shape,
like one of Photis's toy boats.
It is as long as my forearm
but light enough to carry.

It is the only piece of the loom
I will be able to bring.

16.

I find Father at the shore,
toiling over his vats.
I am glad to see him here, at work,
and not stumbling from the tavern.

I ask him to walk with me.
He seems surprised at first,
confused by the request,
but he agrees.

We walk together
along the beach.
It is the first time
we have taken such a stroll.
It is also the last,
for I will soon be gone.

I could leave without a word,
without a trace, disappear
into the night.
But the thought of this
does not sit well with me.
Not after all the loss
he has already endured.

So, I tell my father of my plans,
swearing him to secrecy.

He is a laconic man, sparse of speech—
why should he start gossiping now?

His angular jaw tightens, his face
more unreadable than the sea.

I have learned not to expect
grand gestures of affection from this man,
yet part of me still wonders
if he will miss me. Part of me yearns
for some sign of paternal love
though I know this is a childish wish
that I'm daft to even entertain.

17.

Three days later, when I enter the house
after laying wildflowers on the graves of Mother and Photis,
I can tell Father has come home, but has gone again.

The faint stench of low tide lingers by the door,
along with notes of yeast and yarn,
though there is no hint of sour wine in the air.

A loaf of bread and dried apple slices
sit on the table beside several skeins of wool.

I step closer, blink, freeze.

This is no ordinary yarn: it is Tyrian purple,
dyed the most breathtaking, impossible hue.

I have never seen a color so rich.

The wool alone is worth more
than any sum I have ever touched.

However, I can expand its value tenfold
if I use it to create a tapestry, or chlamys.

My breath hitches;
I am overcome with emotion.

This wool is my father's farewell.

He cannot give me a horse or a carriage
to carry me to my destination,

but this yarn promises
something greater—
    a life
    a future
    a choice
    of my own making.

Words may fail him, but the gesture is clear:
he will miss me. Perhaps he loves me, too.

Though the life we shared
was fraught with hunger and hardship,
I will miss him and our home.

I clutch a bundle of wool
and offer silent thanks.

18.

A memory, ablaze
with color, tinted
with hope and heartache
in equal measure:

Autumn leaves turn and drop,
laying a bright tapestry
upon the ground.

I reach upward, to catch
a fluttering oak leaf
in my outstretched hand.
It drifts and loops,
evading me.

I reach for another, jumping
leaping, laughing.

Again! Photis cheers, toddling
at my heels gleefully. *Again!*

I dash beneath the boughs
until I finally capture
a single leaf in my palm.

I hold it up victoriously.
It glows scarlet and amber,
streaked with gold.

I present it to Photis,
with mock pomp and drama,
like Hermes gifting Perseus
a pair of winged sandals.

Mother indulges us with applause
from her spot along the rock wall.

Photis studies the leaf,
tracing the map of golden veins
with his chubby fingertip.

Then, suddenly, he clenches his fist,
wanting to hold on so tightly
to his prize. In doing so,
he crushes the leaf.

When he opens his palm,
the dry, crumpled leaf breaks apart,
scattering into a thousand tiny pieces.

Photis stares, horrified,
then begins to wail.

I quickly grasp a new leaf
and offer it to him,
but it is no use.

Only Mother's tender touch
and calm voice can halt his tantrum.

You were lucky enough
to catch something perfect,
something whole.

You held it close
then let it go.

Sometimes, that is all we can do.
All we can ask for.

19.

With a sudden rush, I return
from the memory.
I am inside our home again,
wool clasped in my hands.

Outside, a light rain begins to fall,
washing soot and grime
from the stone steps, cleansing
the tidal stink from the air.

Tears streak my face;
I wipe them away.

The purple wool wound
between my fingers
vibrates with color.

I understand Mother's words now
in a different way
than I did as a child.

Even in the wine-dark sea of sorrow
there are small islands of beauty—
          sacred, fleeting, pure.

When your ship comes upon them
throw your anchor and hold tight
for as long as the tides allow.

I inspect the violet strands,
holding tight
to the feelings pounding
in my chest,
knowing these moments
are precious
but they are not mine
to keep.

Then I carry an armful
of skeins to my loom
and cast one final web
across her trusty beams.

In my mind, I hear my father's voice,
Weave it well, daughter.

I shall.

PART III

Weft

1.

Under the cover of night,
Celandine and I don the brown cloaks
I have made for us and sneak
into an unmanned wagon
bound for the lyddite quarries.

We huddle between two large grain sacks,
pull a canvas tarp over our heads, and wait.
We are stowaways, eastward bound.

At dawn's first light,
we hear the voices of men,
the snuffle of horses,
the squeak of ropes tied tight.

I am terrified someone will come back
to check the grain and discover us,
but Celandine assures me
we will not be disturbed,
so long as we remain quiet and still.

She does not say anything more,
and I do not press her,
but I question how she knows this
with such certainty.

I cannot help but wonder
if one of the miners,
            smitten with Celandine,
            plied with a bribe,
has assisted with our escape.

I hope whomever she has conspired with
can truly be trusted.
I fear to think what these men might do
should they discover us.

The horses strain against the ropes.
The wagon wheels shift.
It is too late to turn back now.

With a lurch, we begin to move,
leaving our village, homes, families,
and pasts behind.

2.

I am anxious
about the vast unknown
stretching before us,
the numerous dangers lurking
in these unfamiliar woods.

My mind wanders
to the days prior to our departure,
searching for assurance
that I have not made
a grave mistake.

I may have acted in haste,
but at least I said my goodbyes;
I walked with Father
upon that desolate stretch of sand.

I used the wool he gave me,
pouring a story
across the loom's taut strings,
in rare commune with the women
who wove before—
       my fingers more dexterous than ever,
       the violet thread never tangling,
       the weights balancing evenly—
as though my ancestors
were bestowing their blessings.

I laid one last bouquet of flowers
upon the earthen mounds
where Mother and Photis rest.
My heart ached to leave them,
until the stars overhead
converged to remind me
that mother and son
were no longer beneath the soil
upon which I knelt and wept,
but sewn high above

as glittering sparks of light,
constellations visible not only from Hyponia,
but surely from Colophon, too.

Big bear and small,
so clear and so bright,
with me always.

In this thought
I find peace and purpose.

I exhale, releasing tension
from my shoulders
as I set my mind
to the journey ahead.

3.

The road is rough and uneven.
Celandine grimaces at each bump,
her bruises still tender.

The air beneath the canvas
is dust-choked and stifling.

As the sun rises,
the temperature soars.
I feel faint and sip water
from my jug.

By noon, my bladder is close to bursting.
I clench my thighs together.

Celandine whispers prayers to Hermes,
god of safe travel.
I pray I will not wet myself.

Time limps on.

Finally, the wagons stop
and the men dismount,
scattering into the forest
to gather firewood
and set up their camp.

Now? I ask Celandine,
my voice desperate
but quiet as can be.

She holds up a finger. *Not yet.*

The crunching steps
of heavy boots approach.
My heart races.
Celandine squeezes my knee.

We hear three taps
on the side of the wagon—
knuckle on wood, like a signal.
And then the boots crunch away.

Celandine looks at me.
She exhales, counts to ten,
then carefully lifts the tarp.

The sun sinks low in the sky,
dusk settles over the trees.

The area surrounding the wagons is empty.
The men are busy building a fire
in a nearby clearing.

Now. We scramble out of the wagon
and set off in the opposite direction
of the miners' camp,
finally able to relieve ourselves.

4.

We walk into the night.

Our sandals rub
deep blisters into our heels,
our stomachs grumble with hunger.

My knees and shins ache
as I strain to traverse
the rocky, uneven terrain.

If only I could climb
my way across the valley,
from tree limb to tree limb,
instead of hiking on these
bowed, unsteady legs.

We stop to nibble dried apples
and strips of salted meat.

We don't dare eat too much,
for this paltry stash
must last two days more,
maybe three.

We find a flat patch of earth
and lie down to rest.

Curled together
beneath our cloaks,
we watch as comets
leave trails of light
through the Tyrian sky.

As sleep descends,
our chests rise and fall,
our breath slowing, in sync.

I turn my gaze
from the sky to Celandine.
My eyes wander, wondering at
the topography of her profile,
the slant of her brow, the elegant swoop
of her nose, the dip of her lips,
the curve of her chin,
as though she were carved from stone.

A spark ignites,
spreading warmth
through my chest
and limbs.

While I silently burn,
Celandine shivers.
She pulls her cloak tightly
around her shoulders
and rolls to her side,
tamping out the heat and hope
rising within me.

5.

We awake in the thinning darkness,
startled by the haunting call of an owl.

In the half-light of dawn,
I see the raptor swoop through the trees,
its talons sharp and extended,
ready to snatch up
unsuspecting prey.

We pack our meager belongings
and set off through a stretch
of dense, unknown forest.

I stop several times to make sure
the tapestry I carry rolled on my back
is secure and safe.

I tell a story aloud to pass the time
and to distract myself from
  the pain settling in my knees,
  the worry knotting my throat,
  the flicker of longing I felt last night.

Knot

A story, retold:

*With chisel in hand, Pygmalion could carve a block of stone
into nearly any form. Kings and queens paid great sums
to fill their palaces with his marble amazements:
lifelike lions, muscled athletes, blossoming bouquets.*

*Despite this, Pygmalion was lonely and unhappy.
He courted many women, but none pleased him.*

*As time passed, Pygmalion grew increasingly irritable,
frustrated and disgusted by the bountiful flaws
he believed mortal women possess:
        Too thin, too fat. Too timid, too loud.
        Blemished skin, poor manners,
        unkempt hair, unsweet breath . . .*

*If only he could craft a woman from stone!
Surely, in his deft hands, this marble maiden would be
pure enough, perfect enough, worthy of becoming his bride.
He set to work, carving, hammering, polishing, caressing.*

*Galatea, that is what he called her as her faultless figure emerged.
His passion grew as he imagined the goddess Aphrodite
imbuing his creation with the spark of life,
the girl's cold stone flesh warming to his touch—*

6.

Stop! Celandine interrupts,
halting me in my tracks,
cutting the story short.

She looks from side to side,
squints at the midday sun
angled in the sky, frowns.

We have taken the wrong trail.

Exhausted and frustrated,
Celandine and I quarrel,
our moods bitter and weary.

You led us astray, I grumble,
rubbing my tired joints,
my patience fraying.

Me? She gapes.
*You cannot expect me to know the route
when I've never traveled it before!*

She sweeps her hair from her face
and ties it back in a hasty braid,
the corners of her lips downturned.
*Besides, your constant speech
made it impossible to focus.*

Her words gut me,
but she digs in.

I do not want to hear about a man
carving a woman from stone, Arachne!

I do not want to think of Pygmalion's hands
on Galatea's body, marble or not.

I do not want to learn how he makes her
more perfect than any other woman.

Why must she be perfect? Let her be
whatever she wishes to be!

Celandine storms away.
Her words knock the breath
from my lungs.

How could I be so thoughtless?

I drop to the ground
and pound my fists
on the hardened earth.

The wind rustles
the oaks and laurels,
saying, *Hush, child,*
do not harm your hands.
You will need them
in the days to come.
Do not forget:
they are your tools,
your voice.

But not even my best friend
wants to hear my voice.

I fear the wind
mocks me.

7.

We retrace our steps
in brooding silence
until we find our way.

Finally, Celandine speaks.
I am sorry for lashing out at you.
You did not deserve
the sharpness of my tongue.

Her words chisel
a hole in the dam
that rose between us.

No, it is I who should apologize.
My mood was wretched, I say.
My speech was insensitive and unkind.

A torrent of words
bursts forth
from her lips and mine.

Our nerves were raw,
our bodies tired,
our minds dulled

by the stress and strain
of the journey.

Soon all is forgiven.
We embrace.
My heart swells with relief,
for I could hardly stand
to quarrel with her, the tension
between us more painful
than my swollen joints
and blistered heels.

⌖

We agree to stay near the road
to prevent getting lost, but far enough
into the shade of pine and bramble
to remain hidden from view.

We know how unsafe it is
for two young women
to travel alone, unchaperoned.

Celandine keeps a knife concealed
in the belt of her dress.
I saw the glint of its hilt
when we rose this morning.
I do not know where or how
she procured such a weapon,
but I am grateful for its protection.

Though I hope we will not need to use it.

8.

On our third day of travel,
our food supply runs low.

I touch the tear-shaped vial
that hangs around my neck,
Mother's parting gift.

I am not desperate enough
to drink its contents,
but I like to know it is there,
warm against my skin,
close to my heart.

We find a patch of berries
and eat them as ravenously
as bears waking from winter dens.

Celandine takes one look
at my dirt-smudged face and
berry-stained mouth and bursts into laughter.

I cannot help but join her,
for when I catch my reflection
in a nearby stream
I look as mad as Medea.

We roll in the grass, delirious,
teasing each other,
giggling and tumbling
like children. We stop,
our faces inches apart.

My breath slows.
Celandine looks at me,
red lips parted. Something
flutters in my chest, a quickening
which excites and terrifies me.

I brush a lock of hair from her face,
revealing her eye, still swollen and bruised.
She touches my cheek, the tip of her finger
soft and trembling.

I feel as though I will melt
into the earth, seep down
past the tree roots,
into the molten core. . . .

Celandine bolts upright.
What? I ask, fearing
I have done something wrong.

Shh! She hisses and grabs my arm,
pulling me behind a scrabble of rocks.

Leaves rustle.
A branch snaps.
A man appears.

You there, he says,
stumbling toward us.

Celandine leaps to her feet.
Stay back! she cries,

fumbling for the knife at her waist.
It drops to the ground.
She quickly picks it up again.

Don't move any closer, or I'll ... I'll ...

Please, says the man,
sweat beading his brow.
I am hurt.

He steadies himself against a tree and peels
a blood-soaked bandage from his thigh,
exposing a broken arrowhead
embedded deep within his flesh.

I gasp. Could bandits be hiding
in these woods?
Could this man be a bandit himself?

There is a medical tent down in the camp
where members of our cavalry train, he says weakly.

Celandine lowers her arm,
slides the knife back into its sheath.

Will you help me reach it?
I fear I will die if I do not get help soon.

Celandine and I exchange a look.
Aiding an injured soldier
was not part of our plan.

Leave him, I say under my breath,
tugging at Celandine's sleeve.
We do not need any more trouble.

He is young, hardly more than a boy.
She looks him up and down.
And harmless, at least in his current state.

He tries to rewrap his wound,
but his hands shake.
He whimpers with pain.

Celandine, no. I grit my teeth
as she moves toward him.

What if it were Photis? she says.

My brother is dead, I snap.
Why do you speak his name like that?

I am not accustomed
to feeling so angry with her.
Especially when moments before, we—

We cannot leave this man to die, Arachne.

Why not?
I have no reason to trust him.
I am more concerned
for our own survival.

The camp is not far.
I can see it from here.

Besides, we are headed that way.
She points. Several tents
and makeshift stables cluster
along the valley's lower rim,
bisected by the road to Colophon.

The man moans
and slumps to the ground,
pine needles and leaves
breaking his fall.

Celandine rushes to him.
She cleans the unwrapped wound
with the last of our water
and fixes his bandage,
careful not to disturb the arrow.

Even though I do not understand why
Celandine aids this man, I cannot help
but admire her calm, clear head,
and caring nature.

Thank you, he murmurs.

Help me stand him up, she calls to me.
She throws his arm over her shoulder
and heaves him upward.
She may be slight of frame,
but she is strong.

Arachne, help me!
Stop being so stubborn!

I exhale a frustrated sigh
then join them,
lifting his other arm
up and across my back.

He rises to his feet.
The three of us stumble
and pick our way
down the rocky slope.
With every other step
he sucks in deep, pained breaths.

Finally, we arrive at the camp,
hunchbacked, drenched with sweat,
desperate for water.

We navigate between the horses and fences
and deposit the soldier in the medical tent.

A young nurse greets us.
She looks surprised but grateful.
Set him over here, she instructs, helping us
move the young man to a clean cot.

There is an arrow lodged in his thigh, Celandine says,
gently lifting the bloodied gauze.
I tried to clean it, but . . .

You did well, the nurse says, smiling.

Once the man has been tended to,
she gives us fresh water and stale bread.

I wish we had more. Supplies are scarce.

Thank you, I say. *It is more than enough.*

The generals say war moves this way.
I heard rumors that enemy scouts
were spotted along the mountain pass.

She glances anxiously toward the hillside,
then over at the injured soldier
resting on a nearby cot.
It appears the rumors may be true.
Soon we will need all the help we can get.
Are you here to work? she asks hopefully.

We are headed to Colophon, I explain.
To seek employment in the textile workshops.

She nods. *If you ever change your mind,*
you would be welcome here.

I will consider it, Celandine says,
her face brightened by the possibility.

I cannot blame her;
this sort of work suits her.
But I am surprised, pained even,
by the eagerness in her voice.
Surely, she was only being polite
to the nurse?

We refill our jugs with water.
We still have a half day's walk
before we reach her cousin's house,
assuming we don't lose our way again.

I will not forget your kindness, the soldier murmurs
as we prepare to depart.
May the goddess bless you both.

I nod to him,
but I have little faith
in godly blessings.

9.

The main road to Colophon is thick with traffic—
wagons, horses, travelers on foot.
We feel safe enough to walk in the open,
joining the throng, which flows
like a river toward the sea.

We pass stades of vineyards,
the vines heavy with ripened fruit.
I long to stop and pick some grapes,
but Celandine urges me on.

When we crest the ridge,
a faint breeze tousles our hair.

We breathe deeply, tasting salt
on the tips of our tongues.

The Aegean stretches before us,
turquoise and glimmering,
as far and wide as our eyes can see.

The port overflows with activity.
Trade ships and warships
fringe long-fingered piers,
loading and unloading
weapons and wares.

Fishermen haul nets bursting with fish.
They shout orders and toss ropes
to barefooted dock boys.

In the distance, I spot dye vats,
simmering shellfish and boiling beets.
I feel a pang of homesickness,
until I catch a whiff of their fermented stink.

This way, Celandine says,
pulling me into the heart of the city.

We walk together, arm in arm.

10.

My first impressions of Colophon
are reduced to fragments,
my senses overstimulated, overwhelmed:

The crash of waves,
the creak of wagon wheels.

A shimmer of harp music,
the trill of a lyre's plucked strings.

A brown dog itching with mange,
a gray dog gnawing a bone.

The luster of sunlit marble,
the stretch of shadows cast by columns.

The clack of a horse's hooves,
the bronze glint of bit in its teeth.

The swish of a glossy black tail,
the earthy, hay-tinged scent of manure.

The cry of a baby,
the muffled moans of lovers.

The slosh of water from a bucket,
the snap of laundry hung to dry.

The bitter brightness of citron,
the yellow curl of peels tossed in the gutter.

Out of the chaos and cacophony,
a melody emerges.
My feet on the cobblestones,
the blood pulsing in my ears,
a drumbeat.

The liquid movement of a cat
in pursuit of a rat.

The slap of leather against hide,
the smoke of cooking fires, revived.

The jewel tones of women overdressed,
the stink of rose oil rising from their breasts.

And then, something I recognize.
Something that feels like homecoming . . .

The *husha-hush* of a shuttle
dancing between a weaver's palms.

The faint knock of loom weights.

The whispering whorl
of yarn spinning round.

11.

The textile workshop
is unlike anything
I have ever seen.

Built from massive blocks
of pale, creamy stone
and flooded with light,
the interior practically glows.

More than a hundred women and girls
toil with looms and distaffs,
their bodies in constant motion.

I know none of them,
but I feel a sudden kinship
with these fellow weavers.

Fabric pools at their feet.
Colorful bolts line racks on the wall.

It smells of wool and sweat,
but wide windows welcome
cool sea breezes, making the air
bearable, breathable.

Motes of dust
and bits of fiber
ignite in the sunlight
like flecks of gold.

You! a balding man shouts.

He raps a cane on the stone floor.
The women halt their work.

I was so entranced,
I did not realize I had stepped
into the workroom.

I turn to look for Celandine,
but she must still be outside,
probably wondering
where I've absentmindedly
wandered off to.

The man jabs the cane in my direction.
Who are you? he demands.
And what you are doing here?

I had not planned to seek employment
quite so quickly upon our arrival,
but perhaps if my skills impress,
this supervisor will offer both Celandine and me
a post at one of these fine looms.

I am Arachne of Hyponia.
I have come to work, I say,
unable to mask the nervousness in my voice.

He squints at me.
The women watch and wait.

I am suddenly very aware
of my dirt-smudged face,
my wrinkled clothes,
the unnatural wideness of my eyes.

Can you weave? the man barks.

I look down at my hands.
My nails are short, bitten, unbuffed.
My fingers are not smooth nor delicate.
They are calloused and rough.
They have carded bushels of wool,
spun dozens of skeins,
woven countless cloths.
They are working hands.

Yes, I mumble.
I can weave.

Are you any good? he asks, scowling.

My pulse gallops.
I am not bad, I say meekly,
suddenly awash in self-doubt.

The man snorts, unimpressed.

I wring my hands
and curse myself
for not being more
assertive. For not being
brave enough
to show him who I truly am.

Well? the supervisor growls.
Have you nothing else to say?

My throat tightens,
the words I wish to say
stoppered like wine
behind a cork.

I look down at my hands once more.
They may not be beautiful,
but they are strong and skilled.
They can turn thread into bread.
They can weave grapes so realistic
birds peck at the cloth. This I know.

So I will let my hands
and the work they have crafted
speak on my behalf.

12.

A memory, steeped with color,
sharply focused:

Before I leave my home in Hyponia,
I weave one final tapestry
on my beloved loom
with the thread Father gave me.

Knowing I will need
to sell the work in Colophon,
        a city of opulence
            surrounded by vineyards,
I choose for my subject
a feast of Dionysus,
god of wine, grape harvests,
and ritual madness.

In it, I depict the ivy-crowned god
reclining in a moss-green grotto
surrounded by maenads,
all of whom are far too young
to be his lovers or wives.

I show the nymphs' hesitancy, their discomfort
with the god's unwelcome advances.

Despite their reluctance,
Dionysus does not allow
the nymphs to leave the grotto.

Instead, he plies them
with cup after overflowing cup
of wine, until they dance in ecstasy
and play the tambourine,
nearly naked and fully drunk.
Then, his expression makes clear,
he will do with them
whatever he wishes.

For the tapestry's border,
I weave a twisting grapevine
with delicate curls, veined green leaves,
and bulging clusters
of sumptuous purple grapes
in each corner.

The splashing wine
and glistening grapes
allow me to highlight
the decadent Tyrian purple thread.

I utilize the full spectrum of color,
        from aubergine to oxblood and amaranth,
adding light and shadow, depth and dimension,
with each stitch.

The finished product is so fine
it takes my breath away.

Unlike when I abandoned
Leucothoe's story,
I do not shy away
from weaving or speaking
truthfully.

I have revealed
the ugliness of godly deceit
with near-perfect artistry and craft.
Of this, I am proud.

When I hang the tapestry in my window
to regard the full scene from afar,
hungry birds flock to my sill,
disappointed when their beaks
meet string instead of seed.

13.

I unroll the tapestry
threaded with Tyrian purple
and show it to the supervisor
of the textile workshop.

He appears awestruck—
audible gasp, slack jaw, wide eyes—
but he does not believe
I am its creator.
He even accuses me
of stealing it.

I wish to wear
my hard-earned pride

like a fine robe or shawl
slung boldly across my shoulders,
but his admonishment
strips this joy from me.

You expect me to believe
that a filthy, groveling girl
such as yourself
crafted this masterpiece?
He laughs with derision.
You offend my judgment, child.

Despite my assertion
that the workmanship and ownership
are mine alone, he insists
on administering a sort of test,
requesting that I replicate
a series of stitches
and spinning techniques
while he watches.

I find his demand insulting, denigrating,
but I rein in my emotion
and roll the tapestry carefully back up.

My temper thrums.
My focus becomes
needle-sharp.

Soon he will see
what these hands can do.

⟨∞⟩

The man barks a series of orders.
I acquaint myself with the tools he provides,
greet the new loom, and get to work.

My arms stretch.
My fingers fly.
My confidence grows.

A satisfied smile
tugs my lips.
These rudimentary skills
are child's play.

The supervisor taps his cane,
incredulous and excited
by my speed and dexterity.

His voice smooths
from an irritated bark
to an oversweet cajole.
An eager grin
replaces his scowl.

The other women watch,
unsure what to make of me.
It is unclear if I will be
their competition
or companion.

The supervisor offers me a job,
nearly begs me to accept.

I bask in his praise for a moment,
glad to have proven myself, but
after all this effort, I am suddenly hesitant.

There are other workshops in the city.
I have only just arrived, after all.
Celandine must join me too.
That is what we planned.
I do not wish to make this decision
without her.

I tell him I will think on his offer.

He gapes, then guffaws.
Clearly, he did not expect me to defer.
You'll be back, he says, his scowl returning.

14.

There you are! Celandine catches me by the wrist
as I exit the workshop. Her cheeks are flushed.
I was worried I'd lost you, Arachne!

The concern on her face is so tender, so sincere
that I long to kiss the crease between her delicate brows
and smooth away her worries.

You shall never lose me. My tone is light
but as soon as I say the words,
I sense a deeper note of truth
rooted within them.

Besides, I've been right here all along.
I point to the textile workshop behind me.

As I explain what just occurred, I worry
that turning down the supervisor's offer
was a mistake, that my rashness
might somehow anger or upset Celandine.

But she shakes her head and smiles.
I should have known to look for you
amid the warp and weft.
How quickly you make Colophon home! she remarks,
linking her elbow through mine
and leading me across the bustling agora.

15.

On our way to see Celandine's cousin,
we stop at the market to buy cheese and dates
to bring as a gift of thanks for her hospitality.

But goods are far more expensive
in Colophon than in Hyponia,
and we find ourselves scrounging for coins.

I decide to take out my tapestry once again,
this time to sell it.

A crowd gathers as soon as it is unrolled.
Merchants and tradesmen clamor and bid,
shouting and gesticulating wildly

with their hands. My head swims
with numbers. I cannot think clearly.

Thankfully, Celandine is there to help.
She proves to be a shrewd haggler,
adding the sums, demanding more.
Refusing derisory offers
with a curt shake of her head.

I stare at her in wonder.
It seems Colophon brings out
boldness in us both.

Eventually we sell the tapestry
to a wealthy nobleman.
He is short, with a tall ego.

He wears a tassel-belted chiton,
embroidered with gold.

He licks his lips when he talks,
says he fancies himself to be
as dashing as Dionysus,
with equally good taste
in wine and women.

I almost claw the fabric back, certain
he has completely missed the point.
But when he places a heavy pouch
of coins in my palm, I bite my tongue,
bid the tapestry farewell,
and set off to weave another.

16.

Celandine's cousin, Agatha,
and her husband, Eryx,
welcome us warmly.

Their infant son, Simos,
smiles and coos
from the crook
of his mother's arm.

The family lives modestly;
she works as a laundress,
he as a woodworker.

They offer us a small room
in the back of the house
where Celandine and I can sleep
atop a narrow pallet on the floor.

I am grateful for their generosity
and a place to rest our heads
after a long and exhausting journey.

Before you retire, you must eat, they insist,
setting out the dates and cheese we brought,
along with bowls of stewed lentils and bread.

We dine and talk and laugh.
I feel at ease, comfortable and safe
in their home, in their company,
and in my own skin,

for the first time
in a long while.

I ask Agatha
if I may hold Simos.

There was a time
when I could not
gaze upon a baby
or young child
without feeling
an aching sadness,
remembering Photis,
mourning his absence.

But this boy is sweet and dear,
smelling of milk and soap.

His dimpled knuckles
and gummy grin
soften the hardened parts
of my heart.

I watch as Agatha and Eryx
move about their chores and duties.
They are a loving couple,
balanced counterparts, working in harmony.
Their roles in the household
different, but of equal importance.
They speak to each other
with tenderness and respect.

I find myself longing
for companionship like theirs.

෧ᵔᐟᴐ

After supper,
Simos sleeps in his cradle.

Eryx plays the lute,
Agatha sings softly,
and Celandine dances.

Her lithe limbs sway
to the music.
I am mesmerized
by the curve of her calves,
the flick of her ankles.

She dances as well as Ariadne, doesn't she?
I say to Agatha, delighting in
Celandine's beauty and grace.

Agatha stops her singing.
She lowers her voice.

She dances well, yes.
But it is not prudent
to compare a mortal's skill
to those of the gods,
or even those with divinity
in their blood.

I nod my head, swallowing hard,
hoping I have not offended my host.

17.

That evening
Celandine and I
lie close together
on the pallet
side by side
like we used to do
when we slept
beneath the stars
on the grassy knoll
behind my home.

*Do you wish to have children
of your own some day?* Celandine asks,
rolling to her side.

It is not a question
I have ever really considered,
but I know my answer.

Yes, I think I would, I say,
recalling the warmth and weight
of Simos in my arms.

I wish to love another small soul
the way I loved Photis.
I would like to teach a daughter
to weave, as my mother taught me.

And you? I ask.

Perhaps. She exhales.
Though I am not sure
I am fated for motherhood.

Oh? But you are so good
with little ones. So caring and kind.

Yes, she agrees. *That is a function*
of having many siblings.

There is a long pause.

Arachne? Celandine asks.

Yes?

I have been thinking . . .

I cannot explain why
the tips of my toes tingle.

I await her next phrase,
my mind wandering back
to the woods, to the
berry-stained closeness
of her lips, to the
tapered line of her ankles
as she danced.

I have been thinking
about the camp.

The what? I say,
my thoughts dashed away
like water beneath
a skipping stone.

The cavalry encampment.

Oh? I say, perplexed.

I have been thinking
of the nurse
at the medical tent.

Oh? I repeat,
fighting off disappointment
and a twinge of piercing jealousy.

I would like to learn
about nursing and medicine.
I was always fascinated
by your mother's healing herbs.
Perhaps . . . perhaps I might
pursue training as a nurse or midwife?

She says this like a question,
though she does not need
permission from me.
Still, I wish I could
change her mind.
I wish we wanted
the same things.
My chest tightens.

Questions unravel
like a spool of thread.
I think but do not say aloud:
>   *What about working together?*
>   *In one of the textile shops?*
>   *Like we planned?*

I arrange my face,
construct a marble visage
to mask my feelings.

Quarreling with Celandine, even briefly,
during our journey through the woods
was agony. I cannot risk a fight
that might push her further from me.

You should, I reply, stoic as stone.
Nursing would suit you well.

She peers at me
in the moonlight,
trying to sift
my expression
for answers.

You will not be upset? she asks,
knowing my temperament.
If I do not join you at the looms?

Not at all, I say,
biting the inside of my cheek.
I am not being fully truthful,

but I also want her to be happy.
You should do the work
which brings you joy.

She sighs then hugs me.
Her arms wrap me so tightly
that my heart nearly stops in my chest.

Oh, Arachne.
I am so relieved.
When she releases me,
the warmth of her skin
lingers on mine.

You know I am not
half the spinner you are, after all.

Only when it comes to thread, I reply,
guarding the quaver in my voice.
When it comes to dancing,
you are far superior at spinning.

I can just make out the slant of her lips,
smiling in the darkness.

She rolls onto her back
and falls fast asleep.

I stare at the ceiling for hours
trying to untangle
a messy, stubborn knot.
Trying to make sense
of so many conflicting emotions.

18.

Agatha offers to acquaint us
with the city. Under her guidance,
the dense confusion of streets
and structures unfolds
like a pleated chlamys.

Along the way, I stop to enquire
about work at several textile workshops,
but none are as impressive
as the one I visited yesterday,
with its high roof and wide windows.

In fact, the conditions
in most of the workshops are awful,
each one worse than the next.

Dimly lit with little fresh air,
they are joyless, stifling places,
built for prolific production.

Each one is overcrowded
with miserable-faced women
and short-tempered men
desperate for more weavers.

When I demonstrate my skill set,
they ask me to begin straightaway.

I defer, telling each
I will consider the offer.

I should be happy, but I am not.
For I seek this work alone,
Celandine having made up her mind
to pursue training elsewhere.

This is not the only reason
my heart beats discordantly.

I have only ever spun
in the comfort and quiet
of my own home.

These workshops reduce my craft
to commodity and strip
the pleasure from it.

Then I think of Father's putrid dye vats,
the grueling nature of his days,
and feel a sharp pang of guilt.

I still have several coins
from the sale of my tapestry,
but these are not enough
to purchase a loom of my own.

I tuck them beneath our sleeping pallet
and spend them frugally,
for Celandine and I cannot rely
on Agatha and Eryx's hospitality forever.

I have no choice but to work.

19.

The next morning, I walk alone
to the workshop near the agora,
the first one I visited
when we arrived in Colophon.

You have come to your senses? the supervisor says
when I enter, looking unsurprised.

Last night, I sought Celandine's advice,
for she proved to be a shrewd negotiator
when we sold my tapestry at the market.
She suggested I haggle similarly
for the terms of my employment.

I resisted at first, worried
I wouldn't be able to keep a clear head.
Nervous I would bow too easily
beneath the pressure of rebuke.

But Celandine assured me:
*None are better than you
at the loom, Arachne.*

I smiled at this, for her praise
felt like sunshine,
but also like truth.

Why shouldn't my competence
be compensated?

Well? the supervisor grumbles,
growing impatient.

I have accepted another post, I lie.

His dark eyes bulge.
Then why are you here?
To waste my time?
To insult me? he snaps,
froth flying from his mouth.

No, I reply coolly, determined
to maintain my composure.
To see if you wish
to match the offer.

He sniffs.
I pay a modest wage,
though it's higher than most.
What more do you want?

I plant my hands on my hips,
channeling Celandine's demeanor
when she haggled in the market.

I wish to take a commission
for the pieces I create.

He frowns sourly.
I will give you
ten percent of each sale.
His eyes narrow,

challenging me.
Even that is too generous.

Ten? I balk. *I will take forty percent
and nothing less.*

He blanches.
That is unheard of!

The women in the shop
begin to whisper.

Can you believe her?
     Such gall.
          Audacious.

His ears redden.
He slams his cane
on the stone floor.
Echoes rattle
through the workroom.

*If I agreed to those terms,
all my weavers
would expect the same!*

My eyes drift
from the agitated supervisor
to the women and girls
who pretend not to listen
from their places at the looms.

Exactly, I reply,
suddenly flush and brazen.
They deserve to be paid fairly too.

The women's collective downward gaze lifts.
They blink and regard me anew.

How d-dare you? the man stammers,
detecting a whiff of mutiny
swirl around the room.

*I am happy to take
my skills elsewhere.
The choice is yours,* I say.

My pulse thunders
in my ears.

I walk slowly away,
giving him time
to accept my offer,
or at least
invite me back.

He does not.

*Boldness does not serve
a woman well,* he cautions,
his voice thick with disdain.

I turn and see his mouth
curl into a sneer.

You are a gifted artist,
Arachne of Hyponia,
possessing every skill
except the ability
to know how and when
to defer to authority.

I feel the thorn embedded
in this statement
as sharply as if
it were a spear
driven into my chest.

Nevertheless,
I straighten my shoulders,
fortified by my growing anger.
Thank you for the compliment.

Insolent girl! he spits.
Be gone from my shop at once!

Gladly. I turn to leave,
in earnest this time.

The women stir.
Faint murmurs hiss
like wine poured over coals
at the gods' altars,
the air in the shop
altered.

You will regret this! he shouts,
sensing his reign

over the room,
over the women
diminishing.

20.

I walk the city, stewing.

I curse the world
for cursing girls
who dare to value
themselves.

Is it arrogance
　　　to know your worth?

Is it hubris
　　　to possess confidence
　　　in your abilities?

Is it avarice
　　　to expect a fair wage
　　　and respect?

If you are a woman,
then it would seem, yes.
But if you are a man or a god,
entire epics will be dedicated
to your boldness.

Oh, to be a man.

21.

I sit on stone steps
along the perimeter of the agora,
trying to calm the speed
of my racing heart.

I watch people move through the square.

War-wounded soldiers, leather-skinned sailors.
Mothers with infants balanced on their hips.
Apple-throated young men pushing overpacked carts.

A group of boys squats in a circle,
tossing dice and small, six-pointed sheep bones
onto the ground, cheering as they land.

The wealthy stroll in sumptuously colored chitons,
while sunken-cheeked children beg in rags.

The city is a place of perpetual movement
and stark contrast. I am not sure where I fit
within the fabric of this dizzying place.

But I know the longer I remain here, inert,
the more lost I will become.

I buy a wedge of salty cheese
and a soft fig to restore myself.
I eat hastily.

Then I smooth my unruly hair
and set off in the direction
of another textile shop.

I will not let one encounter
with a small-minded man
dull my spirit
or ruin my chances
at a brighter future.

*None are better than you
at the loom, Arachne.*
Celandine's words again,
echoing in my mind
like an incantation.

Surely, the next workshop
will recognize the value
of the skills that I possess.
Surely, they will offer me
a post and a fair wage.
Surely, all is not lost.

♾

I am turned away
almost as soon as I enter.

No work here, they say,
not meeting my eyes,
nor offering explanation.

I visit a smaller workshop
farther down the road.
The scene repeats itself.

How is this possible?
When only yesterday
you begged me to work?

One by one,
they shrug
and shut doors
in my face.

My burgeoning pride
shrivels like a grape
left too long in the sun.

Only after I exit
the last workshop in the city,
do I fully confront
the gravity of my error.

22.

Celandine discovers me
slumped on the stoop
of Agatha's home,
sobbing into my sleeve.

Oh, Arachne.
What is the matter?

She helps me inside
and listens while I recount
the day's humiliation.

She shrinks from me,
knowing my temper,
fearing I will lash out.

And I do.
I cannot help it.

My emotions explode.
I scream and stomp,
throwing a tantrum
like a petulant child.

This was all your idea! I shout, unloading
my frustration and anger onto her,
whether she deserves it or not.

You misguided me!
We were supposed to do this together!
But it's clear you only needed me
to make the journey with you.

That isn't true,
nor is it fair, she replies.

As soon as we arrived, you left me!
I shake my head, clench my fists.

Left you?
Confusion clouds her face.

You forge a new path
without me, do you not?

She throws her hands up.
We spoke of this!
I asked your thoughts.
I even sought your blessing,
though I need it not.

Clearly. I huff and cross my arms.

Come now, Arachne.
Enough of this foolishness.

Indeed, I must be a fool
to follow you here,
to follow your advice.

Hot tears blur my vision.
I have nothing now, do you see?

Nothing? Her face shifts
at the sound of this word.

Nothing, I repeat, miserably, cruelly.
There is no prospect for me.

You are acting selfishly, Arachne.
Do not place this on my shoulders alone.
Her voice is cold and detached
and it rips my already tattered heart
to shreds.

Do you have any idea how I feel? I cry,
meaning a thousand things at once.
Do you even care for me at all?

She stares at me
but does not speak,
too stunned
or disgusted.
Probably both.

I run to our room
and throw myself
onto the pallet,
refusing to get up
even when Agatha and Eryx
come home for supper.

My mood is wretched.
I would rather go to sleep hungry
than face another living soul.

When Celandine comes to bed
hours later, I keep my back to her.
I fake a snore so she will not bother me.

Then I cry silently
until I fall asleep.

23.

Celandine is already gone
when I awake in the morning.

I rise, sick with regret.

Agatha looks up
from nursing Simos.

She regards my puffed eyes
and disheveled dress.

There is bread on the table, she says.
I am sure you are hungry.

Thank you, I say quietly,
tearing off a piece of crust,
chewing reluctantly,
my stomach unsettled.

Celandine told me what happened, Agatha says,
burping Simos over her shoulder.

Did she recount how I yelled?
How I blustered like a tempest?
How I hurled unfair words?
How she deserved none of it?

I stare down at my feet,
unable to take another bite of bread
or meet her eyes.

There is one more place you could try, she says.

I look up. *For work?*

Not a workshop exactly.
But a place to weave.

If they have looms
and they will take me,

that is enough, I reply,
feeling like a slackened sail
suddenly met with wind.

24.

We arrive at an octagonal hut
with a drooping canvas roof.

What is this place? I ask Agatha,
reminded of the medical tent,
wondering if that is where
Celandine has gone.

It is owned by the palace, she explains.
Staffed with women and girls
who were plucked from their homelands
during last decade's war.

She lowers her voice.
Brought to Lydia
as prizes, chattel, and slaves.
They work here during the day
as spinners and weavers,
creating cloth for the king
and his court of nobles.

Are they compensated
for their work? I ask.

I believe they are paid in mercy alone.
And even that is probably meager.

May I see inside? I ask.

She nods and pulls
the curtain back,
stirring the thick air.

A dozen women and girls
sit bent over their work,
weaving finery in the dim light.

Hello, I say gently, hesitantly,
not wanting to disrupt them.

A young woman looks up.
She is probably a year older than me,
eighteen at most.

She has a starburst scar
on her forehead, perhaps
from the blunt strike
of a sword's pommel.

She rests a hand on her stomach,
swollen with child.

Can we help you? she asks,
her voice tired yet kind.

25.

In exchange for the use
of an old upright loom

to weave my own fabrics to sell,
I agree to aid the women
with their daily work,
which mostly consists of spinning
raven-colored sheep's wool
into seemingly infinite
lengths of soft yarn.

What tint do they employ
to make such a color? I ask,
fingering the strange wool
in the too-dim light.

None, says Myrrine, the young woman
with the starburst scar.

It grows naturally this shade
from a rare breed of sheep,
which the king raises
in pastures outside the city.

I feel a wave of homesickness,
wishing I could show Father
the unusual fleece, knowing
it would interest him.

As I work beside the women,
I begin to feel less alone
and hopeless.

I learn their names—
        Hesione, Elpis, Myrrine.

I listen to their songs and stories—
    widow, mother, orphan.

Slowly, we weave a web
of friendship and trust.

26.

Most nights, I return
to Agatha's home
well past midnight, so
I barely see Celandine.

We sleep on the same pallet,
but she keeps her back
turned coldly to me.
And she rises before dawn
while I sleep until noon.

She no longer smells
of sea brine and lavender,
but of ground coriander,
spicy yarrow, beeswax.

I recognize the scents
of the healing ingredients
from my mother's pestle.

There is comfort and pain
contained within
these fragrant memories.

27.

A week passes.

Celandine and I
have still not spoken.

The distance gnaws at me.
We have squabbled before,
but never like this.

Part of me wishes
she would speak first,
yet I know it is *I*
who must apologize.
To atone for my temper.
To repair what I broke.

I wrestle with what to say.

If my mother were here,
she would tell me to speak
the truth of my heart.

But I fret
that revealing the truth,
        the depth of emotion
        burning within my chest,
might drive her
further and farther
away.

⟋⟋

The longer I wait to speak my mind
and open my heart,
the more difficult and daunting
the task becomes.

Mother used to say
that an argument left unresolved
sours like milk,
turning fouler each day.

Eventually, the spoiled milk
must be discarded;
not even the sharpest cheese
can be made from its soured curds.
Not even the pigs will touch it.

I do not want to throw away
what Celandine and I had together
but I do not know how
to salvage it either.

Just as I was once afraid
to weave the fine yarns Father brought home,
        thinking myself unworthy of their beauty,
I fear that I do not deserve Celandine either.

28.

Distraction is a potent balm,
so I throw myself into my work
with more fervor and focus than ever.

I spin beside Myrrine during the afternoons,
her gentle spirit belying a mountain of strength.
I laugh with broad-shouldered Hesione,
aid nearly blind Elpis with her stitches.

Later, when the women leave the hut
to fulfill their other duties
as concubines to faceless noblemen,
I feel the ache of their absence, and sorrow
for what they must endure.
And, beneath it all, anger, too.

Again, distraction offers respite.
I gather my tools and yarn.

Using my own shuttle—
        the last remaining vestige
        from our beloved family loom—
I set to work.

∞

First, I weave swaddling cloths
and a soft blanket for Simos.

Then, I begin a new tapestry
to sell at the market.
I decide to weave a scene of Colophon
that I hope will appeal to buyers.

I pour my heart
across the warp and weft.

Soon, an image of a beautiful
young woman emerges,
a sprig of gypsophila twirling
between her fingers.

She is one of many faces
tucked within the boisterous city crowd,
but to me, she is the piece's focal point.

In her pale green eyes
I weave warmth,
and forgiveness,
and friendship,
and love.

All the things
I hope I will find
on Celandine's face
when I muster the courage
to speak with her.

29.

When the work is complete,
it must be sold in the market.

Worried I will repeat my past mistakes,
I take my time, observing other vendors.
I study their mannerisms and interactions,
noting which techniques work and which fail.

A woman, it seems, must be firm,
but not too firm. Shrewd, but not too shrewd.

She must raise her voice above the market din,
but she must not be too loud.

She may demonstrate the quality of her wares,
but she must not brag nor boast.

It is a delicate balance
I find difficult to master or accept.

Especially when the other fabrics for sale
are nowhere near as fine as mine.

30.

Finally, I approach a well-known tradesman
in one of the larger shops lining the square,
with many fine goods displayed upon the shelves.

Buying or selling? he asks,
busily scribbling in a ledger.

I swallow and clear my throat.
Selling, I reply.

What do you bring me? the man asks,
sucking his yellowed teeth.

Cloth, I say.
I am a weaver.

He sets his quill aside.
You and every other girl
in this town. He yawns,
looking irritated and uninterested.

This is a tactic
I have witnessed before.
A game I am now
better prepared
to play.

I remain quiet, waiting.

So, you say you can weave.
But are you any good?

It is the same question
the supervisor asked
on my first day in Colophon.

Back then, I could barely
bring myself to meet his eyes.
However, I have grown since that day.

Not only has my craft improved
from hours spent in the weaving hut,
but my resolve has toughened too.

It turns out
loss, disappointment, and pain
can be capable teachers.

The tradesman takes a long swill of water
from the carafe on his table,
awaiting my response.

I said, are you any good? he repeats gruffly.

I straighten my shoulders,
lift my chin.

I am not good, I reply.
I am the best.

He spits, water spraying
from his mouth.
My words revolt him.
My pride repulses him.

He waves a hand to dismiss me.
Get out! he sneers.

I do not leave.
Instead, I untie the leather strip
wrapping my tapestry.

The fabric unfurls
with a dramatic flap.

The cobalt blue edging
catches his eye first.

Then his gaze drifts upward
into the scene I have rendered.
The faces and buildings of Colophon

nearly as vivid as the reality
bustling just outside his shop.

He takes in the details, examines
the fineness of each stitch, marvels
at the play of light and dark.

Do you still want me to leave? I say,
resisting the urge to act smug.

He shakes his head,
beckons me closer.

*I am sure we can strike
a fair deal.*

31.

Early the next morning
I overhear Celandine
speaking with Agatha.

Through the thick stone wall
I cannot make out every word,
but I hear brightness
in Celandine's voice.

She speaks of her work
at a healing sanctuary
within the city walls.
She tells Agatha
about the sick and injured souls
she cares for.

I feel a surge of jealousy,
then realize how absurd it is to envy
these broken, ailing strangers.

Still, I wish Celandine knew
how wounded I am.

I clutch my chest
to see if the rift
widening between us
has torn open my flesh,
for that is how it feels.

Then, I catch the sound
of my name.

I press my ear to the wall
and listen
yet I detect no hint
of remorse or sadness
in her tone.

Our estrangement
must not inflict the same pain
upon her heart as it does mine.

I lie back,
run my fingers
through my hair
and let tears spill
from my eyes.

32.

When I emerge from our room,
the house is quiet and empty.

Celandine, Agatha, and Eryx
are all at their posts,
scattered across the city,
working away.

Even Simos is with a wet nurse
down the lane.

I step outside
into the clear, sun-drenched day.

My coin purse full
from the sale of my tapestry,
I decide to take a short break from my labors
and explore the vine-clad hillside
beyond crowded Colophon.

I watch bees alight on blossoms,
their furred legs fattened
with dusty yellow pollen.

I pick sour apples,
weave a wreath of flowers
for my hair, strolling
through the landscape
like I used to do with Mother.

I inspect a patch of herbs
with silver-green leaves.
I remember how Mother
would fill her basket
with plants like these,
then work tirelessly
to coax medicine, and maybe magic,
from their stems and sap.

I wish I had paid closer attention.
Then I could share
those healing recipes with Celandine
as an offering of peace.

I touch the vial around my neck,
like I always do when I think of Mother,
when I long for her guidance.

I pass a grand temple.
Incense rises from its altar
in heady, smoky tendrils,
but I do not place my wreath
at Athena's feet.
What good would it do?

Later, I discover a mighty tree,
an ancient, gnarled yew.
I am hesitant at first,
for I have not climbed
since Photis fell.
Yet something compels me

and I pull myself up
into its branches.

From my perch,
I gaze out at the world.
The day is warm and bright,
full of color and birdsong,
but somehow everything feels
empty and cold.

Without my family,
without Celandine,
I struggle to find pleasure
or beauty in anything.

I ache for her companionship,
for our conversations, our closeness,
but I am beginning to fear she no longer
values or wants these things with me.

33.

I return to the weaving hut.
As time passes, the women share
more and more of themselves,
spinning stories of their homelands,
sacked, pillaged, plundered.

Nearly all have suffered
unspeakable tragedy.
The loss of loved ones,
brutal rape, horrifying violence.

I do not wince from their tales.
If they are strong enough to tell them,
then I must be strong enough
to honor them and listen.

Sometimes we do not talk,
preferring to work quietly,
bathed in silence,
the small hut filled only
with the softest
      husha husha husha
of our collective
shuttles and spindles.

Today, after a long stretch of silence,
a woman with graying hair
named Drosis begins to sing.

It is a song from her homeland,
in a language I do not know.
Her voice is so clear, so painfully
pure, that it cracks and heals
my heart at the same time.

I am reminded of a story Mother once told me
about a girl named Philomela—
      fellow weaver,
      victim of abuse,
      innocent maid
      turned to lark.

A king abducted her, raped her,
then slashed her tongue from her mouth
to prevent her from speaking the truth.

So she changed into a bird, flew away.

She refused to be silenced, kept singing
and singing, louder, insisting the world listen.

I hear you, I long to say to Drosis
and all the others. *I am listening.*

Selvedge

Pause here for a moment—
       for the poets claim
       there is no story, no glory
       unless women
       weep, crawl, beg,
       submit, succumb, die.

But what of those
       who fight?
What of those
       who rebel?
Who refuse
       to be silenced?
Who think
       with their own able minds?
And speak
       with their own
       sharpened tongues?
Who utilize
       whatever tools
       they have acquired?
Who learn to survive
       no matter what?

Are their tales not worthy
of the poet's prose
or the audience's ear?

34.

When the workday ends,
rain comes sobbing
from leaden clouds,
soaking through the earth.

As I walk the winding road home
my heels leave deep gashes
in the mud.

I think of Drosis
and Myrrine
and Philomela.

Captured and carried
an ocean away
from their families.

It seems as though
an ocean stretches
between Celandine
and me now too.

Its wine-dark depths
too treacherous
to swim across.

Pride and fear prevent me
from building a boat
or bridge to cross it.

35.

When I visit the market next,
I am bombarded.

The tradesman sold my tapestry
to a wealthy family for an absurd sum.
He has been bragging to the other merchants.

> *She is a homely girl, this weaver called Arachne,*
> *But her craftsmanship is impeccable,*
> *the likes of which Lydia has never seen.*

Everyone desires the first look
at my latest work.

The rush of attention
catches me off guard.

The merchants' yelling and hand waving
draws a crowd eager for spectacle,
hungry for gossip and entertainment.

I shrink away at first,
my pulse quickening,
nausea roiling in my gut.

I am suddenly six years old again,
clinging to my mother's skirts,
skittish and unsure.

I want to disappear,
to duck between the stalls,
dart down some empty alley.

You make a name for yourself,
one merchant says,
his tone oblique and opaque.
I cannot tell if his words
hold praise or warning.

Indeed. Quite a stir you've caused,
an older woman quips,
her ruddy cheeks smudged with flour,
her arms riddled with burns from a baker's oven.

I scowl, assuming she chastises me.
Then, she winks.

With that simple gesture,
an ember of pride
reignites within me,
bolstering my confidence.

I push through the crowd.
When I enter the shop,
I unroll my newest tapestry
with a flourish.

A bidding war breaks out
between the tradesman
and the other merchants.

As the men draw fat purses
from their belts, wielding coins
like weapons, my posture shifts,
my nerves settle.

The price soars, my spirit ascending with it.
A rush of excitement washes over me.

When I finally depart,
my pockets sag and overflow,
heavier than they have ever been.

In contrast, my heart is light,
my insides ablaze with the thrill
of the sale, with the prospect
of more moments like this.

I savor the deep satisfaction
that comes with witnessing
the merit of your work
recognized, celebrated.

My confidence and craft
in harmony at last.

36.

Buoyed and emboldened
by my experience at the market,
I resolve to finally speak with Celandine.

With my ample coins,
I purchase a small silver pendant
shaped like a delicate blossom
with a single citrine stone
nestled in its center.

It reminds me of the flower
after which Celandine is named.

I twist several lengths
of deep purple string
into a strong braid,
and thread the pendant
through it.

I enter the house
with the necklace
clutched in my hand.

My palms sweat,
but I will not shy from this
any longer.

I pass through the house,
opening doors, calling her name,
imagining her smiling face
when I present her with the necklace,

longing to feel the embrace of her arms
wrapping around me.

To my dismay,
Celandine is gone.

She was needed at an encampment,
higher up in the northern hills
where fighting has broken out,
Agatha explains, swaddling Simos
in the fresh linens I recently wove for him.

My posture slumps.
Worry replaces eagerness.
It sounds dangerous, I say.
When will she return?

In five days' time.
Maybe more.

My hopes dashed,
my energy quickly draining away,
I slip the necklace carefully
inside my pocket.

Our reconciliation
will have to wait.

In the meantime,
I pray Celandine
will remain safe.

37.

The enslaved women
have little wool to spin the next day,
so I am able to take to my loom
in the daylight.

The rain has stopped
and we throw open
the hut's heavy canvas flaps,
letting fresh air and bright sun
pour inside.

The women ask
what scene I plan to weave
but I do not know.

So far, all I have
is an overly elaborate border
of branches and berries.
It is beautiful but flat,
lacking dimension and purpose.

Summon the Muse! Myrrine jokes.

That bitch never comes to me, I say,
drawing hearty, knee-slapping
laughter from Hesione.

I look around the hut
at each girl and woman,
discovering the inspiration I seek.

I set to work,
finding a rhythm and falling
into a creative trance.

My hands pull, tug, tie
the vision in my mind
to the warp and weft,
thread by thread.

38.

Some hours later,
after the women have departed for the night,
the back of my neck prickles
as though I am being watched.

I turn to find that I am.

Two of the hut's flaps remain open.
Within their frames
several nymphs have gathered.

I startle.

I thought nymphs only dwelt
in wild, natural places,
or in sacred areas alongside gods.
They rarely frequent crowded cities
teeming with mortals.

But here they are,
standing so close

that I can smell
the mossy sweetness
of their breath.

I blink and rub my eyes.

The nymphs gaze at me, at my loom,
lips parted, eyes dewy, hands clutched
to their opulent bosoms.

Don't stop on account of us, they coo,
their voices soft as thistledown.

Why are you here? I ask uneasily.
Their presence is not threatening,
but it is unexpected and unnerving.

We like to watch you work, they reply
in eerie unison.

They wear flowing robes,
the fabric as thin and sheer
as onion skin.

Word of your skill spreads far, says one.

And wide, another adds, a linden blossom
tucked behind her ear.

*We came all the way
from the golden river Pactolus.*

And the vineyards of Tymolus, adds a nymph
with long chestnut hair entwined with grape vines.

What is your name? they ask me.

Arachne, I say, scowling slightly,
wary of their intent.

I've heard the bards sing
of mortals who've gone mad
after close encounters with nymphs,
consumed by unrequited infatuation,
driven to insanity. No matter how beautiful
they may be, I will not allow myself
to fall victim to their charms.

*Where have you been hiding
all this time, Arachne?* they say.

I haven't been hiding, I tell them.
*I just couldn't find work
in the other textile shops.*

Oh! they gasp.
But you are such a fine weaver.

I am, I say, for it is true.
*Those shops are run
by narrow-minded pigs.*

They laugh softly
behind slender fingers.

Has someone sent you to spy? I ask.

No, replies a nymph
with waves of copper hair.
We are not spies.

Not at all.
The others nod.

We are spectators.

I frown. *Spectators?*

*It is pleasing to gaze upon the beauty
of your work, and also to observe
the process of its making.*

Oh, yes, they all agree,
their voices shimmering.

I do not know if I should be flattered,
or afraid. I do not sense malice or trickery
in their voices, but their presence confounds me.

I set down my shuttle
and rub my eyes again,
wondering if perhaps
I am suffering a hallucination.

When I open my eyes,
the nymphs have disappeared.
I am alone with my loom once more.

39.

I finish weaving Philomela's story
as I see it in my mind.

It is a small tapestry,
but a powerful one.

I step back and assess the work;
it may be my best yet.

I bring the tapestry to the market early,
before the street becomes choked
with traffic, dust, and noise.

The tradesman is pleased to see me.
He rubs his palms together
as I unroll the fabric.
He studies it, then balks.

No. He shakes his head firmly,
sucking his teeth.

What do you mean, no? I ask.
Is it not well made?

It is expertly crafted, without a doubt.
Nonetheless, no one should gaze upon
something so gruesome or crude.

He grimaces,
eying the blood congealing
around Philomela's severed tongue,

rendered with shocking realism
in sanguine thread.
It's rather horrid.

Precisely, I reply.

No, he repeats.
*To sell or display such a scene
would surely draw the ire of the gods.*

Well, I say, grasping for words.
*Perhaps the gods ire me
by behaving as they do!*

His nostrils flare.
A vein in his thickened neck bulges.

He reaches across the table
and rolls the tapestry tightly,
eager to be rid of it.

Weave something better next time.

He shoves the fabric into my arms
with an admonishing look,
bringing our conversation
to an abrupt end.

Silencing me
and Philomela
all over again.

40.

The next few days
I stay at the hut,
weaving late into the night.

The tradesman's dismissal of my last tapestry
casts doubt and strife across my work.

I long to create
something meaningful
but I struggle to capture
a new seed of inspiration.

Exhausted, I pause and rest my head
on the loom's frame, feeling the warmth
of the wood grain against my cheek,
savoring the brief reprieve.

Stars glimmer beyond the window.
Insects trill, lulling me toward sleep.

She is tired, a voice says.
You are tired, yes?

I snap my eyes open.
A nymph stands before me once again.

You are tired? she repeats.

I nod, uneasy.
I glance around
to see if she is alone.

Then you must rest.
For soon you will have
a larger audience.

A second nymph emerges
like a specter from the darkness.

Yes! She claps excitedly.

An audience? I say, stunned,
wondering why they have returned.
What? Why?

I receive no reply,
for the nymphs have already gone,
drifting as silently into the night
as they arrived, leaving only
the faint perfume of linden blossoms
and a thousand unanswered questions.

41.

I return to Agatha's house,
eager to tell Celandine
about my strange encounter
with the nymphs. Then I remember
she is still far away in the hillside camp,
tending to injured soldiers.

An arrow of regret
punctures my chest.

Her absence in this small room
feels impossibly large.

I sit on the edge
of the pallet we shared.
I touch the place
where her head should rest.
I picture her there,
sleeping soundly beside me,
her face in the moonlight
smooth as poured milk,
her chest rising and falling
in such peaceful measure.

More than anything,
I long for her to return.
I long to speak with her,
to hear the warble of her laughter,
to feel her shoulder bumping gently against mine
as we walk through town, remarking
at the life we're building here together.

I reach into my pocket
to check that the necklace
of silver, citrine, and braided string
remains safely nestled
within the fabric folds.

When I finally see her next
I will admit my mistakes
and make amends.

I resolve to be stronger,
braver. Less afraid
to bare my heart.

A vow to myself:
      When Celadine sees me again,
      she will find me transformed.

42.

I sleep restlessly,
tormented by nightmares.

A thousand tales converge
      in my head   distorted dreams
          and jumbled myths bleeding
into each other
      woven edges fraying
          tapestries unraveling
              re-knitting
      hardening   into fragments   shards
          mirrored obsidian   shattered   sharp as knives
palms in prayer
          crumbling temples
              unrequited love
      sea-tossed shipwrecks
          salt-bleached beaches
      an archer's bow releasing   a misguided arrow
burning stars   funeral pyres
          a swallow returning home to its nest
      a silent-winged raptor
          perched upon a fence post
      a serpent twisting   constricting . . .

I gasp for air and bolt upright,
awake, covered in sweat,
thrashing at my sheets
like Heracles wrestling
the snakes sent to kill him
in his cradle.

43.

I arrive at the weaving hut at dawn,
eager to escape the dark and nightmares.
Hoping for a few quiet moments
to clear my head before the day's work begins.

However, the nymphs are already there, waiting.
And there are more of them.
Many more.

Why are you here? I shout
as I open the hut's flaps.

The weaving women
look up from their work.

Not you, I say, shaking my head,
flustered. *Them.*

I point to the crowd of nymphs
gathering around me
in their diaphanous robes.

Hesione and the others
shift uncomfortably on their stools,
unsure what to make of the scene.

Your fame rises like smoke.
A doe-eyed nymph sighs,
her pupils black and shiny as polished stone.

*Such is the loveliness
of your art, Arachne,* says a long-haired one
I recognize from last night.

You ply me with compliments, but why? I demand,
shaking out the hut's canvas flaps,
feeling as though I cannot breathe,
in desperate need of air.

*Because we admire your craft.
And we are not the only ones.*

In the distance, people gather—
        noble men and women,
        street children, fruit sellers,
        fishermen, midwives, and more.

They move like a clot
toward the weaving hut.
I can hear the low rumble
of their voices.

I taste bile
as panic rises.

Here they come, says a nymph,
linking arms with another.

We have sent for them
and they are here,
just as the goddess requested.

The goddess? I stutter.

Weave for us, Arachne! the nymphs instruct,
as though I am a bard
about to perform a great ballad.

Yes, you must, another insists,
in that maddening, lilting tone.

The mob is upon us now,
an eager, excitable mass;
there is no hiding.

I turn to look at the women,
my friends and companions in this work,
but they are as dumbfounded as I.

Hesione shrugs.
I suppose you should weave then, girl.

44.

I sit at my loom, command
my hands to stop shaking.
I pick up my shuttle
and find comfort

in the familiar heft
and shape of it.

I close my eyes, open them,
take a breath,
and begin to weave.

I have no nymphlike grace
or delicately sculpted features,
yet the crowd sighs
over the deft movement
of my hands,
my speed and skill
perfected over hundreds,
probably thousands, of hours.

My shoulders relax
as I find my rhythm,
passing the shuttle,
tying the threads.

See how nimbly she works? someone remarks.

*How lucky to possess
a gift from Athena!* another gushes.

*Clearly, she learned
from the goddess herself.*

I stop. I turn on my stool
to face the nymphs
and townspeople.

Their words goad me.

The goddess did not teach me, I say,
color flushing my cheeks.
My mother did.
As her mother taught her.

I see faces in the crowd frown,
displeased with my retort.

I may be as skilled as Athena—
oh, mighty goddess of weaving—
I mutter sardonically,
but she gifted me nothing.

A collective gasp.

The nymphs' pretty mouths
gape stupidly like fish
pulled from water.

Whatever skills I possess
were wrought from hard work,
heartache, and sacrifice.

Nothing was handed to me.
Nothing! I cannot hide the irritation
in my tone or the fury
expanding in my chest.

I have always struggled to contain
my temper; now that it is unleashed
it is impossible to restrain.

An old crone hobbles forward.
She wears a gray headscarf.
Her skin hangs from her bones.
One of her eyes is clouded with cataract.

You, girl! She shakes her cane at me.
You truly claim to be as skilled
as the goddess herself?

I stand and nod.
Why should I lie
and say I am not?

She clucks her tongue
on the roof of her mouth.
You'll bring the wrath of Olympus
upon your head
if you keep that up, foolish girl.

Do not chastise me, old woman.
I throw my shoulders back.
You know nothing
of the struggles
I have endured.

A breath of wind
swirls at the hems
of the nymphs' dresses.

Clouds collect in dark swaths
across the morning sky.

Believe me,
I would have gladly accepted
Athena's guidance and gifts,
if only she had appeared.
I throw my arms wide.
She never did!

I look out at the sea
of riveted faces.

How many of you lay offerings
at the feet of the goddess,
to no avail?

Nervous chatter ripples
through the crowd.
Most are too pious
or afraid to reply,
but a few hardened faces
nod knowingly.

My skill was born
out of a need to survive, I tell them.

I did not have the luxury
of waiting for Athena
to present herself to me.

The old crone cranes
her wrinkled neck.
You wish for the goddess
to present herself to you? she croaks.

Yes, why not? I reply,
my voice loud and clear.

The crone recoils,
bellowing, *Offer prayers!*
Atone! Impudent girl!

I will not! I shout.

Thunder rumbles.

Then prepare to face the ire
of the goddess herself!

Fine, I say. *Let her come to me!*

45.

The crone's headscarf falls away.
Her clouded eye brightens,
flashing with silver.

Her wrinkled skin tightens and smooths
as her hunched form straightens,
growing taller and taller
until she towers over me.

The cane becomes a spear.

A crack of lightning ignites the sky
in a jagged seam, searing the earth
beside the golden sandals of Athena.

She holds my gaze, her eyes like a vise,
rendering me immobile. I hardly breathe.
Despite my disillusionment,
there is no denying the awesome might
of the goddess towering before me.

She clangs the shaft of her spear to her chest.
The gleaming aegis she wears across her breast
produces a sound like the roar of dragons.

The air shifts. The wind blows colder.
An owl screeches and alights on Athena's shoulder,
its yellow eyes studying me like prey.

My pulse thunders in my ears.
Shock slowly thaws to fear.

The nymphs sway,
bristling with terrified delight.
The townspeople shudder and gawk.

The ground shakes with the power
of a thousand pounding feet,
but only one approaches: Athena.

You summoned me,
and now I am here!

My ears ring.
I have never heard a god speak.
Her voice is like a waterfall,

tumbling and immense,
deafening in its strength.

Atone and bow to me,
insolent mortal! she commands.

Perhaps it is stubbornness,
perhaps it is strength,
but as frightened as I am,
I will do no such thing.

I have a name, I say, placing a hand
upon the nearest loom to steady myself.

The goddess squints at me, narrowing
her gray eyes to knife-edged slits.

You have a what?

A name, I stammer.
I am Arachne, I say,
finally finding my voice.

I know who you are, she replies,
as though she's been following me
for quite some time.

Then you know
the quality of my work.

You dare insult me, Arachne? Athena booms,
practically spitting my name.
Lowly mortal, you overstep.

My life suddenly seems impossibly small,
dangerously fragile, as easy to stamp out
as an insect beneath a foot.

Instinctively, I touch the vial at my neck,
hidden beneath the cloth of my dress.
I try to recall my mother's wisdom.
But she never prepared me for this.

Then I remember a question she posed
during our walk in the woods,
the night we harvested the moly:
> *What makes a god afraid, Arachne?*

I had not known the answer.

> *A power greater than their own,* Mother replied.

I leave the memory behind
and return to the weaving hut,
to the crowded square,
to Athena before me.

I take a breath,
root my feet to the floor.

I only speak the truth, I say.
If that causes insult,
then it is a reflection of you, not me.

Careful, mortal, she warns,
her tone thick with condescension.

My mother's voice again:
> *Guard your anger wisely, Arachne.*
> *Gather it like a precious herb,*
> *for there may come a time*
> *when you will need to draw*
> *great strength from it.*

If there were ever a time,
it must be now.

I feel it then—this alchemy of anger—
powerful, empowering,
coalescing into courage.

I am as skilled a weaver as you, I declare.

The crowd trembles.
Athena's angular jaw tightens.
She grips the spear, her knuckles white.
Oh, really?

In fact, I may be better.

The nymphs clutch their breasts,
quivering at my reckless audacity.

Is that a challenge? Athena asks,
her eyes playfully cruel,
like I am a mouse and she a cat
who plans to bat me around for sport.

It is, I reply, gathering
all the mettle I possess.

You dare to challenge me? Athena—
goddess divine, daughter of Zeus,
inventress and protectress of the craft itself—
to a weaving competition?

Fortified by years
of carefully cultivated anger,
I lift my chin. *I do.*

Her laughter crackles
like pork fat in a hot pan.

Then let it be so!

46.

Athena raises her spear.
A bolt of lightning
strikes the ground—
Once! Twice!

The nymphs and villagers
jump back and scream,
shoving each other out of the way.

The air smells of burnt hair
and sandalwood.

Where each bolt struck the earth,
two huge looms appear, baskets of fiber
in every color imaginable at their sides.

You wanted a challenge,
so a challenge you shall get, Athena proclaims.

My vision blurs, my head spins.
I must focus. I must shake away
the doubt and fear scraping
and howling all around.
I must harness my anger.

I pick up my shuttle
and walk stiffly to the loom
that has materialized
before me in the square.

It is robust, finely built,
rubbed with olive oil.

Athena takes her place
at the other loom—
an incomprehensibly massive oaken frame
that is somehow dwarfed
when she stands beside it.

A team of oxen would struggle
to carry such a load,
yet she summoned and assembled it
with the flick of her spear.

Etched bronze plates reinforce each joint,
and the freshly polished wood glows.

The onlookers murmur excitedly.
I follow their gaze and discover that
Athena's loom weights are gemstones,
magnificently faceted rubies and emeralds
that glint extravagantly in the sunlight.

With a pang, I remember my humble family loom,
the one I was forced to leave behind
when I fled Hyponia. I can hear the arthritic creak
of her old boards, reclaimed
from my grandfather's fishing boat,
kissed with circular sea-marks,
softened by sand, salt, and time.
Honored by my grandmother's hands,
my mother's, and mine.

Athena's loom may be extraordinary
but it could never compare to my own.

The goddess's booming voice
wrenches me from the memory.

Craft your finest tapestry, she commands.
And I will craft mine.
Then, proud Arachne,
let us see who the victor shall be!

The nymphs whisper breathlessly.
The crowd surges forward,
jostling for the best view.

I gaze into the basket by my feet,
overflowing with the most sumptuous
silk, flax, and wool I've ever seen.
There are even skeins of what appears to be
spun silver and gold. Sparkling,
impossibly delicate, yet strong and supple.

There was a time
when I would have shied away
from such exquisite materials,
convinced I was not worthy or capable enough
to do them justice.

A flicker of memory,
like a song trapped within a shell,
a faint echo, my father's voice:
  Weave it well, daughter.

I reach into the basket,
grasp a bundle of Tyrian purple.
The violence of violet
seems an auspicious choice.

Emotion surges and swells
as I imagine the color seeping
through my skin, infusing me
with its potency.

Slowly, meticulously,
I wind the shuttle with fresh yarn,
giving myself a moment to plan.

The sun beats down.
My heart thrums.
Athena glares.

When the shuttle is wound,
an eerie calm washes over me.

Across the square,
I meet Athena's expectant eyes,
steely, unflinching, unafraid.

I grip the shuttle tighter.
There is no turning back now.

Let us weave, I say.

And then we are off.

47.

The poets, when they tell this part,
choose the vocabulary of war.
For once, they are not wrong.
It is a battle and we are warriors.

I gird my loins, sharpen my weapons,
armor myself. Attack.

I bind the threads to the beam
sketching a scene in my mind,
my hands barely keeping pace
with the speed of my thoughts.

Over and over, warp and weft,
I draw strands from left to right,
but my shuttle slips clumsily.

I am rattled and awkward.
I stretch my arms and wrists.
Perspiration beads my brow.

I catch a glimpse of Athena.
Unlike me, hunched and sweating,
she sits rod-straight and relaxed.

With a single tap of her finger,
entire rows of thread weave themselves
into wonder. I grit my teeth
and vow to keep my eyes
on my own loom.

I take several deep breaths
to calm my nerves.
Then I set to work again.

I feel the shape of the shuttle
in my hand. I touch the loom's beam,
listening. I balance the weights—
roughly carved stones, not glittering jewels—
that hang along the bottom.

I build up more speed,
bolstered by the familiar
husha husha husha

of the shuttle passing
through the strings.

When I press the loom too hard,
I hear my mother's voice
whispering in the breeze:
> Patience, child. Do not rush.
> Do not waste this moment.

It strikes me
how important this is.
Beyond appeasing
ego or pride,
this is a chance
to speak out.

To spin the finest yarn yet.
To reveal the truth.
With all of Colophon
watching and listening.

48.

I adjust my movements and fall
into a more natural cadence.

I become a blur of motion
and color and wool.

Forms and patterns
emerge in the tapestry
as my awareness

leaves me, a sort of trance
seizes me. I lose myself
in the loom. I find myself
in the loom. I become
the loom.

I swim through seas
of deep Ionian blue,
fields of pale celery,
petal pink, lyddite black,
saffron yellow, Tyrian purple.

Relying solely on muscle memory
and instinct. Everything I require
is already stored within me, locked inside,
honed over countless hours,
waiting for this very moment.

In the hazy corners of my mind,
I sense the sounds of cheering,
raucous hoots and slapping palms,
as though this competition
between Athena and me
is as entertaining as a wrestling match
or chariot race.

I tune out the noise.
I work and work and work
until I no longer feel
my fingers,
my hands,
my arms,

my legs.
I am pure
creative energy.

I think, maybe,
I am flying,
like Icarus,
dangerously
close to the sun.

49.

Somewhere, a horn blares.
The deep, lingering call
of air blown through the hollow
inner spiral of a conch.

The roaring crowd,
the goddess,
the yarn,
come back into focus—
      sharp and sudden—
a burst of light and sound
rushing at me
with such force that I jolt
from my stool.

My finished tapestry
fills the loom's expansive frame.
It is more striking than anything
I have ever created.

The threadwork is impeccable,
the play of colors and glints of gold
a delight for the eye.

But what I have chosen
to illustrate, to illuminate
within the tapestry's center
is most powerful.

⚬⚬⚬

Behold! Athena crows,
silencing the crowd.

With the snap of her fingers
(unblistered, uncalloused, I note)
Athena's loom swivels round
to face the rapturous eyes
of the crowd, which has grown in size.

All of Colophon, maybe all of Lydia,
has gathered to watch us duel.

Athena's face is silver-smooth and smug.
She is used to commanding
an audience, accustomed to
adoration and attention.

She displays her tapestry
with detached interest
and easy confidence.

Her work is a florid glorification
of the twelve Olympian gods.

Aphrodite, Apollo, Zeus
are radiant, just, mighty,
and capable of punishing anyone
who crosses them.

Cautionary scenes bloom
within the tapestry's four corners,
depicting the unfortunate fates
of mortals who dared
to compare themselves
to the rarefied gods—
        Antigone, Rhodope, Haemus, Gerana,
          turned to mountains, cranes, ugly-beaked storks.
There is no subtlety
to Athena's message.

Her composition is symmetrical:
four corner scenes, a border, and centerpiece.
For the privileged few, like gods and kings,
the universe is a place of order and balance.
It is pleasant enough to look at, but flat,
lacking tension and movement.

Athena has woven herself
into the center of the tapestry,
basking in her triumph over Poseidon
in the contest for Athens.
Shield and lance in hand,
her aegis guards her heart and breasts.
Where her spear strikes the fertile earth,
an olive branch sprouts.

I am reminded of Narcissus,
gazing upon glassy water,
delighting in his own reflection.

And you, Arachne?
Athena addresses me.

What have you made? she asks,
her voice cloying, calculating.
I hope it will impress. . . .

I raise my chin.
It will not disappoint.

With the flick of her wrist,
the loom turns,
revealing my work
for all to see.

50.

Unlike Athena's tapestry,
my work tells a very different tale.
There is no order, no symmetry.
No balance, nor fairness.

Each finely woven length of yarn hums
with scintillating beauty,
but the scenes I have rendered
are raw and real. Often ugly.

I have chosen to depict a combination
of my mother's myths and my own life,

stripping away the poets' gilding and lacquer,
revealing the stories of Leucothoe, Philomela,
Callisto, Antiope, Danae, Melantho, Alcmena,
Galatea, Erigone, Demeter, Aegina.
I show myself, Myrrine, Hesione . . . and Celandine.

The centerpiece of my tapestry exposes
two dozen incidents of deception,
assault, mutilation, and rape.

Violent, lurid, inexcusable acts
repeated over and over again
with barely any consequence.

Exacted upon innocent women and girls
by Kronos, Helios, Poseidon,
Dionysus, Amphitryon, and Lykos.

I name them all. I show their faces.

I owe these gods and mortals no special treatment.
I owe the women everything.

I show Hades abducting Persephone,
Apollo molesting Daphne, and
Zeus—Athena's own father—
taking the form of a swan to penetrate Leda,
an eagle to violate Asterie,
a bull to abuse Europa.

Europa looks back to the shore—
        at the crowd of people who now study the tapestry—

her face pained, frantic, as she screams for help.
The rising seawater surges around her feet.
Make no mistake, she is not being seduced or wooed.
She will be raped or she will drown.
Will we do anything to stop it?
Will something finally change?

51.

My work is flawless.
This is not flattery; it is fact.

My tapestry entraps the crowd's gaze.
They cannot look away or hide
from these awful, all-too-common truths.
And I know they will not easily forget.

I hope they will never hear
the bards' songs and the poets' prose
quite the same way again.

I hope those with power
will feel shame and regret,
resolve to be better, and
hold one another accountable.

And when more vulnerable voices
bring their own stories to light—
however brutal or uncomfortable
their individual truths may be—
I hope they will be believed
instead of blamed.

52.

Athena roars, striking the ground with her spear,
sending deep, angry reverberations
through the stones beneath our feet.

She has been defeated.
The villagers, the nymphs,
everyone knows it.
Athena knows it too.
But she does not like it.

She strides toward me,
her gray eyes sparking with rage.

Insolent, impudent mortal! She seethes.
How dare you show such disrespect?

She casts her gaze upward
at swirling charcoal clouds,
as though the eyes of many gods watch us.

Do you know who you offend? she hisses
through gritted teeth, her nostrils flaring.

Do you? I ask defiantly.
I gesture to my loom.
Do you condone these abuses?
Do you deny them?

She stiffens, sets her jaw.

You of all should understand, I add.
I remember the tales my mother told.

"Athena the Virgin," they call you.
Not an easy title to maintain, is it?

She bristles at the epithet.

Especially when Hephaestus
tried to rape you? He failed, of course,
but can you not recall the terror
of his advance? His unwelcome
hands on your flesh?

She fumes. Thunder claps;
fierce winds howl.

Can you not empathize
with the women I weave? I press further.
Can you not bring yourself
to defend them?

Her eyes flash. I am surprised
she does not speak,
or strike me down.

Did you ever think to stand up
to your father, mightiest of all Olympians?
You never rebelled against him, but why?
Rumors suggest that you could be greater than him.
Have you ever wondered if it might be true?

Her grip on the spear tightens.

Legend says your aegis is so strong,
Zeus's thunderbolt could not pierce it.
The prophecies have not come to fruition;
the dreaded son, the only one capable
of Zeus's demise, never manifests.

She winces. It is the faintest gesture,
a fleeting slip of emotion.
The crowd does not seem to notice.
If I were not staring at her face
so intently, I would have missed it too.

Maybe the prophecy is wrong, I say to Athena,
my voice softer now, less combative.
I pick up my shuttle and offer it to her, in truce.
Maybe it was meant to be a daughter.
Maybe it was you all along.
Maybe it still can be.

53.

The force of her blow
dashes the boxwood shuttle
from my hands.

My head throbs with pain.

I misread the signs,
interpreted her wrong.
So very wrong.

I scrabble after my shuttle
on my hands and knees,
cradle the cracked wood
in my palms, the last
relic of my family loom.

Like a storm,
Athena is upon me.
Her cruelty springs
quick as weeds.

How dare you speak
of the gods so brazenly!
Your disrespect
will not go unpunished, lowly mortal!

She summons the wind.
Undo these evil threads!

Angry gales dismantle and destroy
the greatest work of my life,
shredding the tapestry
into tattered pieces.

The nymphs wail.
The crowd shrinks away.

The warp strings snap,
one by one, twanging
like a poorly tuned lyre.

Athena raises her spear
and smashes the loom to pieces.

Heavy timbers snap like twigs.
She hurls them effortlessly
across the square.

Villagers scream and duck.

She rips the shuttle
from my shaking hands
and takes aim.

The blow lands
with such force
that my vision flares,
my ears hum.

Again and again
the shuttle crashes,
splitting my skin
until the white of bone
shows through the red.

I stagger to my feet
and try to escape,
drunk with pain and delirium.

Athena squints scornfully.
Where do you think you're going?

I don't make it far
before a fierce wind knocks me backward.
I stumble, collapsing to my knees.

One last coherent thought:
    How did I expect this to unfold?

A mortal who refuses
to back down,
to look away
from the sins of the gods,
never meets a pretty end.

This, the bards always get right.

And yet, despite the gash on my head,
the throbbing behind my eyes,
the ruined tapestry and broken loom,
I would do it all over again.

54.

Arachne! a scream disrupts the haze of pain.

I know that voice.
I lift my head,
force my eyes open.

Celandine pushes through the crowd.

She kneels beside me.
She presses her palm to my head,
to slow the bleeding.

The sight of her
bellows my lungs with air,
dulls the ache of my injuries.

I am so sorry, I say, fighting back tears.

Quiet now.
Celandine cups my face
in her hands tenderly.
I am here.

No, I say, shaking my head,
sick with the thought
of Athena harming her.

I look up frantically.
Sure enough, the goddess moves toward us,
her shadow on the flagstones
as sharp as her spear.

I use my remaining strength
to push Celandine away.
You must go. Please.

You wish me to leave? she asks, anguished.

No, I reply, my voice thick with emotion.
*I wish nothing more
than to be with you.
Always. In every way . . .*

*Then let me help you.
I will not let you die, Arachne!*

I swallow, wincing in pain.
*I will not let her hurt you.
Go! Please,* I beg.

I lock eyes with Celandine,
trying to convey all the things
I feel inside. All the things
I should have said sooner,
hoping she understands.

Dark rivulets of blood
trace down my face.

I reach into my pocket
and pull out the necklace
I purchased for her.
The small yellow stone glows
in the waning light.

I set the silver blossom
into her open palm,
close her fingers,
stained with my blood,
around the petals.

Let us be sewn in the stars,
like Andromeda and Perseus, I say,
recalling her favorite constellation
from our childhood days. Confessing
something I have never before
been brave enough to reveal.

Celandine's eyes grow wide.

Athena's shadow draws nearer,
her footsteps louder.

Go, I plead, depleted,
my voice hoarse and desperate.

I don't want to leave you, she sobs.
I cannot lose you, Arachne. Not again.

You shall never lose me, I tell her,
repeating the words I said
on our first day in Colophon,
when I wandered into the workshop
and we were briefly separated.

Look for me amid the warp and weft.
You will always find me there.

She blinks back tears.
I hope she will find solace
in this promise.

Celandine slips the necklace
over her head. She clasps my hands,
squeezes them tightly.

The ground beneath us rumbles and shakes.
Step aside, meddling mortal! Athena booms.
Or you shall face my wrath too!

Go! I scream.

Two nymphs suddenly appear beside Celandine.
They grip her by the arms, their willowy frames
belying unexpected, inhuman strength.

Celandine kicks and wails,
trying to break free, to return to my side,
but the nymphs pull her away
into the dense crowd
before Athena can punish us both.

55.

Athena stands before me,
her eyes burning like a brand.

I will give you one more chance.
Atone for your hubris and disrespect!
Repent. Beg forgiveness
for your abominable creation.

My head pounds.
Anger coats my throat.
Resilience and determination
course through my veins.

If I were to repent now,
what would that say
to the people gathered around us?
To the enslaved women I wove among?
To Celandine, and all the others who deserve better?

I will not deny or degrade their stories.
And I refuse to dishonor my mother,
who entrusted me with so many of these tales.

I look up at Athena. I never imagined
I would encounter, let alone confront, a god.

For a single moment, I wonder if I am asleep,
deep within another twisted nightmare.

No. I am awake and alive.
I cannot waste this moment.

Admit that you despise my work
because you fear my work, I say.
My tapestry was a mirror
showing an ugly truth.

Brow furrowed,
dark hair shimmering,
chin thrust boldly out,
she delivers a numbing blow.

I slump to the ground.
My mind goes hazy.
I will not relent, not yet. . . .

You can destroy my work, I rasp,
clinging to consciousness.
But you have not won.
It is too late.
The world has seen.

The crowd susurrates.
I can barely see them anymore,
but I sense them all around.
The people, their faces.
Eyes watching, ears listening.

Once told, a story
cannot be easily erased, I say.
It takes on a life of its own,
growing, reproducing.
A story is immortal.

Immortal, yes.
Athena pauses.
Unlike you.

56.

I am no match
for Athena's wrath,
especially when she aims to kill.
Of this I am certain.

But I am stubborn to the end.
I decide, then, that only I
will defeat myself.

I roll to my side,
turn my back to the crowd,
and plunge my hand
down the front of my dress.
I reach for the glass vial
I keep hidden, close to my heart.

Pause here—
    There is a cord
    around my neck, yes.

But be wary:
it is not the noose
most bards describe.

It is thin, braided,
encircling my skin—
        a memory of my mother,
        an amulet imbued with magic.

I tug the cord. There is no time
to consider the vial's contents,
or to work a stubborn knot.
I snap the fibers
and the vial comes free.

I recall my mother's dying words:
        Drink this
        and make a wish.
        New life begins
        where another ends.

I uncork the vial,
part my lips.

The moly's power
remains a mystery,
but deep in my heart I know
this is the last remaining option
to control my own destiny.

The sharpened tip
of Athena's spear

glints brutally.
The myths all agree:
the goddess never misses.

I quickly empty the tonic
into my mouth,
tasting decade-old herbs,
currants, moss, clove, and smoke.

Will my mother's pharmaka
still work? Did she ever possess
real magic at all?

Slowly, painfully, I rise to my feet.

Athena's owl screeches.
The goddess circles me,
ready to flay the flesh
from my body,
eager to impale
my beating heart.

I do not cower.
I will not
bend my knee
to pray or beg.

I will meet my fate
standing tall.

I lift my chin
wondering

if Helios watches
from the domed sky above,
reveling in the demise
of yet another mortal girl.

My vision flares,
white, hot, blinding.
And then I feel it—
        not the gruesome slash of Athena's spear—
something else entirely.

A faint tingle in my gut.
A bubbling, spreading warmth.
I am overcome
by a heady lightness, as though
I have enjoyed one too many
cups of wine.

I blink, trying to regain my sight.

Athena has paused her attack.
An odd expression passes
across her livid, luminous face.

The villagers watch
in captivated silence.

My muscles spasm,
my toes curl.
I cry out,
a deep, primal scream.

The empty vial falls from my hand,
shattering onto the stones.

57.

My scalp prickles.
I scratch. A clump
of long black hair
falls to the ground.

Horrified, I scratch again
and the rest of my hair follows,
scattering at my feet
like a mare's severed mane.

Athena regards me
with flinty, unreadable eyes.

The tonic I swallowed
wells up. I stumble
and retch, emptying
the contents of my stomach
onto marble temple steps.

The crowd gasps
at my irreverence.
To defile an altar
is crime enough,
but to do so
in the divine presence
of the goddess herself
is unthinkable.

I cannot help it.
My body convulses.
I heave and hack,
trying to rid myself
of the poison
I have ingested.

58.

Time must have soured
my mother's tonic.
Surely, she meant to gift me
a less excruciating exit,
not something as vile as this.

Pain comes in unrelenting waves.
I'm afraid I may have made
a terrible mistake.

I consider Athena's spear
and find myself almost longing
for its swift relief.

The goddess stands, rigid as stone.
She shows no mercy,
only a strange fascination,
riveted by my suffering.

A grating, high-pitched noise
pierces my ears.
The sound burrows
into my head,

splintering my skull
like an axe, cleaving away
all logic and reason.

A scalding itch
ripples across my skin.
Blistering boils
swell and rupture.

I shriek and spasm,
writhe and wail.

I fight and resist,
but agony
overtakes me.

I scrape at my flesh,
wishing
I could shed, molt,
tear myself
free
from the confines
of this mortal body
and crawl away
to safety.

59.

As soon as the wish is made,
my spine arches.

My muscles seize, my teeth clench.
I bite straight through my tongue
then gag on the metallic taste
of my own blood.

I buck and fall to the ground,
limbs splayed grotesquely.

All the while, Athena watches.
The crowd is still.
No one attempts to aid me.

This is probably best;
I am too far gone
for saving.

See what happens
when a girl grows too proud?

My bones snap and dissolve,
re-forming from the outside in.

See what happens
when a woman dares to act
as confident as a man?

My belly distends.
My eyes bulge.
Fangs rupture my jaw.

See what happens
when a mortal
disrespects the gods?

My arms and legs
shrivel, then multiply.
I sprout thousands
of short, dark hairs.

See what happens
when Arachne—

Enough. Please.

I have given my life for truth.
There is nothing left
to give.

I finally succumb
to white nothingness.

PART IV

Unraveling, Again

I
am
no
longer
in
pain.

I
am
free.

I
am
calm.

I
am
peace.

I
am
light.

I
spin
and
spin.

I
am
dizzy.

So
very
dizzy.

I
fade
in
and
out
and
in
and
            out. . . .

&

How much time passes?
An hour? A day?
A year?

I float
weightless
suspended
by gossamer silk.
            Or rope?

I cannot tell which.
Perhaps the bards were right
all along.

Perhaps I am dead.

If not, then I am
on the razor-edged brink
of life, hanging on
by a thread.

᎒᙭᙭᎒

A woman's face
comes into focus.

Not a mortal woman.
Nor a nymph.
A goddess.

It is Athena. Ah. Of course.

She is here to deliver
my final punishment.

Though her fury has morphed
into something stranger.

She cocks her head,
transfixed, bewitched.

She is much larger
than I remembered.
Much, much larger.

She flicks the string
from which I hang,
sending vibrations
through my body.

The string, I realize, attaches directly
to my abdomen. How very odd. . . .

She brings her face close to mine.

I meet her gaze.
Somehow my vision is keener
than it has ever been.

My mouth moves
but I make no earthly sounds.

In the reflection of her
gleaming silver breastplate,
I see myself—
          my new self.

          New life begins
          where another ends.

The strange alchemy
of Mother's tonic
deformed me.

No, it did not deform me.
If transformed me.

For I am not damaged
or incomplete.

I am still Arachne.

But now
I am a spider.

Grotesquely beautiful,
beautifully grotesque.

Amid the chaos and confusion,
a strange kind of peace
settles over me.

Athena picks me up,
cups me in her hand.
Now she will squash me,
her size one hundred times
my own, at least.

It does not matter.
After everything I have endured,
I am not afraid.

My eyes—
          there are several of them now—
meet hers.

She pinches me
between her fingers.

Holds me up
for the nymphs and villagers
to observe.

The crowd murmurs.
My story, my very own myth,
already burning on their lips,
ready to spread like brushfire.

Despite the mortal Arachne's
unforgivable transgressions,
and unbecoming hubris,
I, mighty Athena, will show
this repulsive creature mercy.
Though we all know
she deserves nothing!

The goddess puts on a show,
spinning a tale
of disappointing falsehoods.

She tells the world
that her powers caused
my transformation.

With my back turned,
the crowd did not see me
imbibe the tonic, so they accept
her words as truth.

Except for Celandine,
none could have known
that my beloved mother was so much more

than she seemed, her mastery
of witchcraft powerful enough
to rival the abilities of gods.

Athena pretends
this transformation
     from girl to spider
was meant as punishment.

But we both know the truth.
I changed *myself.*

I try to speak,
but my mouth is too small.

Go! Athena commands,
lifting me high for all to see.
You are condemned to hang for life!
Doomed to weave for eternity!

Her cruel laughter echoes
throughout the square.

She releases me
onto a tall marble sill.

Before I scurry away,
she leans close, whispering
so that no one else can hear,
Spin, Arachne, spin.
And seek justice
where you can.

The crowd dissipates.
They chatter rapturously,
telling, retelling,
mistelling my tale,
adding flourishes
and stretching the truth
like the metalsmith
who pulls and hammers
molten bronze until it shines.

The square is nearly empty now,
except for a flaxen-haired girl
who moves through the wreckage
of torn tapestry and unraveled spindles.

Piece by piece,
she collects the splintered shards
of the boxwood shuttle.

She falls to her knees
in the middle of the square,
clutching the broken wood
to her chest.

She hangs her head.

A young woman with a starburst scar
and a stomach swollen with child drifts to her side.

She touches the flaxen-haired girl
gently on the shoulder.

She presents her with one last piece
of shattered wood.

Celandine looks up.
Thank you, she says softly.

Did you know her? Myrrine asks.
Arachne, the weaver?

Celandine's pale green eyes are wet.
Yes, she replies, wiping them dry.
I loved her.

Cutting Ties

I cling to the walls,
ascend the rafters,
and hide from sight,
my legs trembling
as the reality
of my new life
sinks in.

I find strange consolation
in the words my mother spoke
so many years ago,
on the day of my first menses,
when I changed
from child to woman:

> *Transformation*
> *is often painful, Arachne.*

> *But there is power to be found*
> *in your new form.*

New Looms

In time, the shock of my fate fades.

As a mortal,
my resolve was already toughened
to exoskeleton from a lifetime of hardship.

My incisors sharpened
from speaking my mind.

My legs bowed since birth.
My arms adept at climbing.

My hands and heart most content
working with thread.

And so, the more I consider it,
becoming a spider
is an almost natural progression.

I find myself oddly comfortable
inhabiting this new form,
spinning, weaving, hunting.

It is, perhaps,
the most at home

I have ever felt
in my own skin.

Though I do spend
uneasy hours
contemplating
Athena's parting words.

Was that remorse
I detected in her voice?

Could she have felt
some degree of regret?

How should a creature
as small as me
offer justice
to an unfair world?

Sooner than expected,
an opportunity presents itself.

Gossamer

The dawn is new,
the roosters just waking.
I'm nestled in my latest web—
a magnificent spiral
bejeweled with dew,
spanning the upper eaves
of a tavern in the city square.

A young woman
in a cream linen dress
and flowing black hair
carries a basket of eggs
toward the market.

A man materializes
from the shadows,
smelling of musk and wine.

He has been watching her,
perhaps even following her.

His tunic is finely woven.
A belt of tanned leather
strains against his barreled form.

He approaches.
The girl pauses.
They speak.

I can tell
from the nod of her head
that she knows him,
or recognizes him, at least.

Something about him
is familiar to me, too.

I cannot make out
the words they exchange.
Even if I could,
my ability to comprehend
human language diminishes
with each passing day.

Even so, I understand the signs.

I have many eyes,
one of the sundry benefits
of becoming a spider.
With them, I see
everything.

The man's expression shifts.
He steps closer—too close,
his eyes burning
with predatory fire.

If I could,
I would shout, *Run!*

Instead, I inch along the roofline.
Eight legs give me
unparalleled agility
and for this I am grateful.

The girl slinks backward,
trust dissolving into
alarm, shifting to fear.

The man glances around,
to make sure they are alone.

He pulls her
into a dim alley,
shoves her
against the nearest wall.

He presses one hand
across her mouth,
rendering her silent.

Her basket drops.
The eggs crack,
yellow yolks leaking
across the dusty ground.

The girl's chest
rises and falls rapidly,
as the man slides

her hair aside,
kisses the nape
of her neck.

A small, terrified sound
escapes from behind
his suffocating palm.

The air is acrid
with sweat and distress,
wine and lust and greed.

I descend from the eave
silently, small as a mote of dust,
deadly as a sharpened spear.

His hand moves
from her horrified face,
downward.

I cast my line,
deftly drift, then
land, unperceived,
on his shoulder.

Careful now, I tell myself.

The girl spots me.

If I still possessed
a human tongue
I would say,

Hush!
I am here to help.

Instead, I look at her
with my plentiful eyes,
imploring her
not to scream.

Her lips quiver
but she does not cry out,
perhaps sensing
I am friend, not foe.

The man's uninvited hands
roam across her body;
there is no time to waste.
This injustice
must end now.

I climb up his tunic
until I meet
a sliver
of exposed skin.

I am so close
but then—
he moves violently,
grabbing at her skirts.

I catch myself
from falling
with a delicate

but strong thread.
I hang on tightly
until I can find
my footing again.

The man grips
the girl's wrists,
wrenching them
behind her head.

I must move faster.

She inhales sharply,
which the man mistakes
for pleasure. A sly smirk
creeps across his face.

A pale pink scar
puckers his left eyebrow.

Without hesitation,
I sink my fangs
into the flesh
of his neck.

I release my poison,
count to three—
      1 . . . 2 . . . 3 . . .

It takes another three seconds—
      4 . . . 5 . . . 6 . . .

for the man to register
the sting of my bite.

His face contorts.
He releases
the girl's wrists.

He slaps a thick, sweating palm
to his neck, to kill
whatever pest
he imagines
has bitten him there.

But of course
I am long gone.

I watch safely
from the roof
high overhead,
having already departed
soundlessly, stealthily
on my silken string.

My venom courses
through his veins now,
its potency building
with each portentous second.

His face slackens,
his complexion pales.

His knees give out.
He slumps to the ground,
his whole body
weakened, flaccid, failing.

He groans.
This is not the lustful utterance
of an appetite sated.
It is the sound
of death approaching.

The girl watches.
She is shocked and scared,
but safe.

Before fleeing,
she casts a grateful gaze
in my direction.

⁛

My work is done.
          For today, at least.

I retreat to the shadows.

I groom and preen,
tasting iron and salt,
blood and sweat.
All the complex flavors
of revenge.

This brings little satisfaction
and I wish to cleanse my palate.

So I spin for myself a new web,
and assume my rightful place
in its tensile center, awaiting
more appetizing prey.

Selvedge

Moons wax and wane.
Tides rise and fall.
Crops sprout, ripen, wither.

All around me, the world shifts.
I welcome its cyclical rhythm
as I prepare for change of my own.

I fuss over a small white sac
where I carry hundreds
of unborn daughters and sons.

When they hatch,
I will greet them, teach them.

       Spin, my children, spin.

       Spin webs.
       Spin stories.

       Use your thread
       to lift each other up.

       And bite back
       when you must.

I will weave for them
a great tapestry of my life
so that they may know
who I truly am.

Acknowledgments

Writing and revising a book during the height of the pandemic while homeschooling two small children often felt like a Herculean task, but it was made possible thanks to the following divine beings:

Many thanks to Allison Hellegers, agent-warrior extraordinaire, for being a fierce advocate of my work and a genuinely delightful person. I'm so grateful for your vision, encouragement, and friendship. Thanks also to everyone at Stimola Literary Studio for nurturing creators and making dreams come true. Gratitude of Olympic proportions to Julia McCarthy for seeing the potential in Arachne's story. Your infectious enthusiasm, impeccable insight, and editorial witchcraft are unrivaled. Heaps of appreciation to all the fabulous and hardworking folks at Atheneum/S&S, including Anum Shafqat, Jeannie Ng, Sonia Chaghatzbanian, Irene Metaxatos, Penina Lopez, and Elizabeth Blake-Linn. Tremendous thanks to Deb Lee for creating beautiful cover art, and to Joy McCullough, Colby Cedar Smith, Kip Wilson, and Cody Roecker for such generous blurbs.

A pantheon of talented and patient people helped me transform a scraggly manuscript into a rich and layered tapestry of a novel. Thank you to my writing colleagues, mentors, critique partners, and dear friends for reading countless drafts, offering honest feedback, and keeping me motivated, especially Erin Cashman, Diana Renn, Sandra Waugh, Rebekah Lowell, Krista Surprenant, Steff

Higgins, Stephen Anderson, Rajani LaRocca, Susan Lubner, Sarah Glenn Marsh, and Elaine Dimopoulos. To Pat Barker, Natalie Haynes, Francesca Lia Block, David Elliot, Madeline Miller, Jennifer Saint, Nikki Grimes, Jeannine Hall Gailey, Julie Berry, Roshani Chokshi, Nina MacLaughlin, Elana K. Arnold, and many others—your poems and stories healed, inspired, and uplifted me. Extra-special gratitude to Julie Taymor for reintroducing me to Arachne, serendipitously, by way of *The Lion King* musical. (Yes, you read that correctly. Inspiration often travels circuitous, delightfully unexpected paths.)

Heartfelt appreciation to all the teachers, librarians, and booksellers who have supported my journey so far. I gathered strength, wisdom, and awareness from Katy Waldman, Jia Tolentino, Miranda Schmidt, Dr. Christine Blasey Ford, and Chanel Miller. I consulted a wide variety of Ovidian interpretations while researching this book, including the work of A. D. Melville, Charles Martin, Allen Mandelbaum, Arthur Golding, and Rolfe Humphries. I'm particularly grateful to Professors Emily Wilson and Stephanie McCarter for offering fresh, vivid, accessible translations of ancient texts, as well as opening my eyes to the deceptive and sometimes harmful nature of euphemism.

Much like Louise Bourgeois's striking spider sculpture is an ode to her *Maman*, this book is dedicated to my own beloved mother, weaver of stories, protector of nature, poet, and so much more. My father read the earliest draft and told me this was the book that would change everything. Thank you for always believing in me.

To my radiant daughters, may you continue to be strong, creative, and kindhearted. I am so proud of the young women you are becoming, and I am forever grateful to be a part of your stories. To Stefano, my partner in each epic odyssey. And my homecoming, too. You are my star-sewn love.

At its core, Ovid's *Metamorphoses* (which includes Arachne's tale) explores the concept of transformation. Fittingly, researching and writing this book was transformative. And cathartic. A much-needed outlet to channel deep rage, vent frustrations, and contemplate complex dynamics of power, pride, trauma, and speaking out. During a time when so many of us find our basic rights under attack, our bodies more regulated than firearms, our voices repeatedly silenced or ignored, Arachne's story feels more timely than ever. To all the readers, writers, survivors, and storytellers, I hope this book honors you.